I0527714

Full Throttle Cyborgs

TOO HEMI FOR YOU

LANDRA GRAF

Too Hemi for You
ISBN # 978-1-80250-544-3
©Copyright Landra Graf 2023
Cover Art by Erin Dameron-Hill ©Copyright May 2023
Interior text design by Claire Siemaszkiewicz
Totally Bound Publishing

TOO HEMI
FOR YOU

Dedication

To my forever friends.
I keep going on this journey because of you.

Chapter One

The weights were heavy, and Hemi Finster was surviving on pure determination not to let Shannon down. *Not that she's coming back.*

Sweat beaded on his forehead, and he grunted as he pushed on the bar driving the round weights at either end upward. The muscles in his human and cybernetic arms burned. He shouldn't have cared so much about a woman he barely knew, but then again, his post-surgery hired nurse had been the only one who hadn't treated him like something fragile or broken. *It's their damn fault I'm this way to begin with.*

"You've got this," Gina said on a low note. She shouldn't have needed to be here, but Hemi knew damn well she carried guilt for what happened to him. *More than anyone else does.*

So when he needed someone to spot him or work beside him in case anything went wrong with his physical therapy since Shannon had left, Gina was always the first to volunteer.

He embraced those words and let out another sound, more like a low roar, as he pushed the weights up. Gina then held the bar with one hand and put it on the hoists.

"Perfect. Great job. That's ten reps today and you're almost not straining. I bet in a week we can move up to thirty pounds on each side. I can get Snapper to bore another hole in a chunk of Marsanium. Not like we're using it for much else besides sludge."

Hemi sat up and took the proffered towel from Gina with his human hand. He refused to voice the truth — that sheer willpower had gotten that last rep in. He'd been so close to letting the weights fall on him. "Let's not rush things."

No, no rushing...because as much as part of him wanted behind the wheel of a racer, another deep-seated voice told him to run. Run as fast as he could to escape whatever the future held, or drown himself in drink until he couldn't remember the racer blowing up, his body on fire, then passing out from the agony. The pain had been so acute that sometimes he could swear the nerve endings of the left side of his body were still on fire.

He'd fought against those insidious ideas over and over as he tried to gain control of the new parts on half of his body.

"Of course not." Gina offered a jug of water. "I'm just excited to see you doing so well. You're sticking to the regimen Shannon provided, and even after they've been gone a few days, you're still doing everything she said."

"Yeah." He took a long swallow of water then mopped at his head and neck again with the towel. The fast difference in the experience of moving was upsetting. He could feel the rough, absorbent material of the towel, but the jug in his metal cybernetic hand was a cold nothing.

His life was filled with this half-existence now.

"I'm going to head out since that was the last rep. Promised Snapper I'd help him finish some test runs..."

Gina trailed off. He couldn't stop staring at his metallic hand gripping the jug— a slight bit of pressure and he could crush the metal construction. Except he wasn't sure how much strength to use or how long he could last before his hand would fail him.

"Have a good night and tell Snapper I said hello." He tried his best in these moments to summon the expected responses, forcing himself to interact with others for the seemingly mundane sense of normalcy.

"What about you?"

"Dinner at the Watering Hole, as usual. Gaia's doing something new tonight, a recipe she got from a traveler. It's something called a dumpling."

"Ooh, yes. I'll remind Snapper. We wanted to try those as well. Maybe we'll see you there."

Hope not.

"Sounds good." He set the jug on the floor and stood, draping the towel around his neck. Gina appeared to believe his movements implied he was in a good enough state to leave.

Her hovering was nice, to a point. But as the metal door to the makeshift workout room clanged shut, he let himself plop back on the workout bench. Everything there, the metal frame, the uprights holding the weight bar and the weights themselves rattled.

His hip ached, and he didn't miss the little bit of dizziness that remained due to his weight differential between the human body remaining and cybernetic components.

He was training to extend the stamina of his cybernetic parts, gain control of their strength and increase his human body mass to offset changes the cybernetic parts exerted.

Fuck. He could easily lie back on the bench and not bother moving, but if Gaia didn't see him walk through the Watering Hole doors in the next hour, she'd send someone to check on him.

He snapped the towel off his neck and tossed it across the room, the only physical manifestation of his frustration.

Full Throttle was the reason he'd been given a shot at being a driver to begin with and without them he wouldn't be alive, which was the thought that propelled him off the bench and to his house. He washed up and avoided looking at himself in the cracked mirror.

A half hour later, Hemi felt as ready to face the crowd in the Watering Hole as he could. He spent a good ten minutes debating on walking with his cane or without. The Marsanium rod in his hand provided a tiny bit of security, just in case.

His stomach growled repeatedly as he made his way to the building. Old wood panels pressure-sealed against metal plating, the wooden boardwalk, the covering and the repainted sign in bright black announced the Watering Hole to anyone who passed by. The wind had died down a bit from earlier so minimal red dust wound through the air, enough that he didn't need to cover his face. The sunset in the distance cast a deep red glow across the entire town. The buildings looked as if they'd been painted in blood, a visual that brought memories he didn't care to recall.

When he opened the door to the bar, the rush of voices, musical notes, the clink of glasses and laughter hit his ears. Here he could forget about his problems for a minute as those from the gang who gathered were good at focusing conversation elsewhere. He basked in the smell of hops and wheat brews along with mouth-watering spices and the heavy scent of yeasty bread.

"Hemi, you made it before I had to send a minder," Gaia called out to him as she filled two mugs with house brew and passed them off to one of her helpers.

"You mean a minion? What did I say about needing regular checkups?"

"My workers are always happy to escape for a minute during the evening rush, so think of it as doing them a favor."

A favor, my ass. He warred between appreciating the gesture and hating the threat to his independence with a passion. Since the accident, he'd barely been left alone, yet here he was deliberately seeking out a busy place because drowning his veins in alcohol appeared the best way to stave off the nightmares that might creep up on him.

"Here's the stew with the dumplings. If you want more, just ask. And the brew." Gaia set down a mug and bowl with a wood-carved spoon. "Enjoy."

Then she was gone, her long, pale-blonde braid swinging as she turned and moved to the next customer at the bar. Though that was where Frog Lick differed from every other gang-town. No one had to pay, even non-gang-member customers. Food and brew were always free if a person was in the bar. Money didn't exchange hands unless someone wanted something other than house brew, usually recycle or any type of alcohol with more bite.

Drag, their fearless leader, believed in giving sustenance to everyone in town. No one deserved to starve, ever. The community, the gang, lifted each other up. Free food for anyone. Where some of the larger, stout members might have been greedy in other gangs, eating three to five servings of anything they could have, people in Frog Lick never took more than two servings, to help ensure there was enough to go around.

Hemi grabbed his items and moved away from the bar to clear space for the next set of arrivals. Usually, he sat up front near the stage, listening to the music from the local guitarist, Privy. But tonight, he opted for a table closer to the door. After the long day, he wanted to eat and drink, then get out.

Snapper and Gina most likely wouldn't show. Drag was out with his brother, Rune, and Petal, Rune's wife. Jack…well, Jack and Hemi's hired nurse were off on a mission to save him and his fellow cyborgs.

Chasing solutions to cybernetic degradation. I was saved just to be destroyed again.

That supported the idea of having another drink instead of rushing home. Who knew if Jack and Shannon would even be successful? If they weren't, his days were numbered, and he'd much rather spend them in distraction.

"Hi, Hemi." One of the many single Frog Lick ladies slid an arm around his shoulders, while another sat in the chair beside him.

Both women wore grins and a provocative glint lit their eyes. That was about where their similarities ended. Josie, with her auburn hair and her freckle-covered skin, and Haimea, with her rich black waves and dark sienna tones, were the exact opposites of each other in every way, except they were both hardcore dust honeys.

"You're looking good. Maybe those cybernetic parts will help in the next race?"

He wouldn't be behind the wheel any time soon. "Maybe. What brings you lovely ladies to my table?"

The pair glanced at each other, then at him. He tried to take all of their admiration in stride, tried to pretend he enjoyed Haimea snaking her tattooed hand across his pant-covered cybernetic thigh, though he couldn't feel a thing. Therein lay the problem—even though these ladies continually offered themselves to him, Hemi couldn't bring himself to disappoint them. In times past, he'd enjoyed the sexual overtures of both ladies and even their sensual enthusiasm. They found pleasure with each other as much as they seemed to delight in sharing him.

"We were thinking it's been a while since you had us over."

"Uh-huh." Josie leaned in closer with her lips at his ear, her red locks draping over his shoulder. "We miss that delicious mouth of yours."

They missed what he could do for them, but he wasn't capable of such things anymore. At least not in the sense of full involvement. It was possible to engage in the use of his mouth without other parts of his anatomy. If he truly wanted a distraction, they would provide it.

"Well, I'm happy for a reunion."

"That's not all we want…"

Josie kept talking, but Hemi found himself distracted by the opening of the Watering Hole door. It creaked as it was spread wide, lingering sunlight from the setting sun shining into the darker room, kicking up a haze of red dust. For a second, it looked like the entrance was on fire. Then she walked in, pale-blonde hair whipping around a slender tan neck, greenish blue eyes that reminded him of the saturated chem pools that the Uppers drowning in flash swam in. He'd once known a person who had one. She had the same look, same graceful walk, same — *Fuck.*

And just like that, his past had walked in the door. Hemi stumbled to a standing position, unsure if he should run toward a woman who always seemed to turn up in his life at the wrong time to hug her close and thank whatever higher power existed.

But as fast as she appeared, she whisked right back out of the door and it slammed shut.

Hemi was still in a state of shock. He blinked rapidly, wondering if he'd seen a mirage or if this was the start of the degradation. "Ladies, I think I may need to call it a night. We can pick this up tomorrow."

Both women pouted, their lips dusted in a pink glitter that reflected tiny sparks at the slightest hint of light. He had no desire to appease them and whatever distraction he'd hoped to find was lost the minute he'd dreamed of seeing a part of his past.

"You promise?"

He did his best to summon a grin that would rival the way he used to smile at the women. "Have I broken one yet? Tomorrow."

They both came to either side of him and pressed their lips against his cheeks, leaving their mark, before giggling and walking off to find the next male driver or mechanic willing to entertain them. Though drivers were slim picking with Jack gone and Drag retired — he was the last one.

And there's not much left.

He pounded back the rest of his beer, left the empty mug on the table then headed for the door. Once on the porch, he turned to the left, using his cane to help support his weight. Since he'd been sitting, his human side was even more worn out than earlier. The trip to his makeshift home, the one Drag had gifted him when he'd joined up with Full Throttle, would probably take longer than it should. Though home wasn't the same without — *her*.

This time she had a hood on, but he didn't miss those eyes or the way her long, pale-blonde hair cascaded over her shoulders, the sensuous yet agile way she moved. He'd often likened her to an angel with tan skin and a piercing gaze that could either make one melt or wither.

"Hemi?"

His name sounded more like a question from her lips. He was so screwed. It looked like his past had just caught up to him, and it wasn't leaving without a reckoning.

Chapter Two

Two hours earlier

There were three things wrong with Sophia Archer's current destination. One, the Osprerine gang lived in burrows. Their mounds of packed dirt were nothing compared to the glittering three-story rises her people had built among the trees that littered swaths of Aurora Terra, the third colonized region of Mars. Sophia preferred a life aboveground.

Two, she had no love or emotion for the man her parents had determined would be her husband. In fact, she could barely recall his name.

"How do I address him again?"

"Caden."

She glanced at her dear friend and bodyguard, Teija, who sat to her right, scanning the horizon. "How is it you remember his name crystal clear and I have no clue?"

Three, she had barely spoken to this man she was supposed to marry and was walking into a situation she had no control over.

He was silent for a minute, but Teija always took time to consider his words. Without sparing her a glance, his mind obviously focused on his duty, he clicked his tongue. "Because I find it's important to know the names of possible people I may have to hurt."

"Hurt? I'm supposed to marry him. I don't think my father will forgive you if you ruin my chance at a perfectly good alliance between gangs." Sarcasm was etched into her words, and she couldn't help but feel a little sore at the future she faced.

She wanted to lead her people, her gang, not be relegated to taking up a position with some foreign group that would require her to navigate a whole new world of social expectations. Osprerine would be a different life altogether and she despised giving up her dreams for her parents and antiquated traditions. She'd already given up her heart's desire based on her parents' wants. *Why do I have to sacrifice more?*

"Your father wouldn't, but you would. May I speak plainly?"

Sophia let out a soft snort. "Uh, last time I checked, you never asked my opinion."

"There's a first time for everything and you appear extra sensitive today."

She hit Teija on the arm, a playful slap with no real force behind it. "Thanks. Spit it out already."

"You can make this your own adventure. It doesn't have to be all about what they want. Remember to do things for you."

Right then she saw the glimmer of a metal roof in the distance. The distinctive flash was a reminder of a gang-town she'd heard of. Full Throttle was where Hemi had gone and where he'd almost died. *Of course, I'd think of him right now.*

"Do you truly mean that?"

Because she wasn't due in Osprerine for another day or two. She could take this time to do exactly what her friend suggested. *Live for myself. Just see if he survived.*

"What did you have in mind?"

"Maybe a detour?"

Teija glanced in the same direction but didn't respond right away. "If that's what you want."

Sophia nodded. She wanted a chance to see if he'd lived, and if he did, to see him without the shackles of her family's expectations hindering her.

"Then let's go to Frog Lick." She pointed in the direction of those metal roofs. The sun's reflection was bright enough to make Sophia put her hand up over her sun-goggle-covered eyes as if the extra shade would reduce the glare.

Teija directed their driver to point the hauler in that direction and away they went. For the first time in days, Sophia felt a little lighter, buoyant and somewhat anxious. Because what if she got there and found Hemi… *What then?*

She believed he was still alive but wasn't sure. The rumors from the accident had spread throughout the regions, from one gang to the next. Stories about Full Throttle and their quest to save their driver by converting his body with cybernetic tech.

Tech that several other members of the gang had been equipped with years before, courtesy of a sponsor alliance. Yet those were only rumors. Nothing had been confirmed as most of the gangs in her region had limited contact with those from others until the championship race.

She'd only been at the regional race because her father had been seeking a husband for her, looking for an alliance. The crash still lived in her memory…their last conversation.

"You may not find what you're looking for." Teija's statement brought her out of the memory trail she'd been chasing.

"True, but better than no answers at all. I still feel guilty he's out here. Maybe if I hadn't…"

Teija's low grunt had her trailing off. He was her staunchest supporter and despised it if she even implied blaming herself for anything. "We all make choices. You're not the sole reason he left or the one who caused that explosion. I was there, too. NiteOx is dangerous. Everyone knows Full Throttle was experimenting and therefore Hemington knew the risk."

"Those are rumors, Teija." She swiped a few of her long blonde locks behind her ear, even as the wind whipped more of her hair into her face.

"Not a rumor when the paperwork and official review was conducted by the Mars Racing Commission."

She tried to ignore the shock, but she had a shit poker face. *Probably why I get in so much trouble.*

"You didn't know?"

No, because she'd been too busy fighting fist and boot against her parents' commitment to marrying her off to Caden of Osprerine—the son of the current Osprerine gang-town leader and, with their marriage, the future leader of her own gang, Aurestral.

"It's been a busy couple months. Let me have this chance to forget what my future holds and a moment to be a woman who wonders what happened to the man she once thought the world of."

Her friend was the embodiment of stoicism, sitting straight and tall, as he stared straight ahead toward Frog Lick. "I wouldn't tell everyone that. You might spark questions from your fiancé."

"He hasn't even officially proposed." Sophia sighed, the exhale representative of the weariness in her soul. She was being dramatic, sure, but all her work at making friendships, understanding the delicate balance between being one of the gang and the leader of the group, had effectively been put to waste by her parents' decree.

She balled her fists against her thighs, allowing the tendrils of her hair whipping in the wind to obscure her vision.

"He plans to." Teija had spoken with Caden on behalf of her parents in the initial conversations. Not her.

"Nice of you to know more about my fiancé than I do. I haven't spoken more than three words to him."

He gently shoved her with his shoulder. "Don't. It's gang tradition, not a slight against you."

"Woman don't talk business. They talk distraction." Her mother's own words were spoken every time Sophia had wanted to pursue a future that directly involved her using her voice.

"That may not be the intention, but I'm hurt all the same."

Teija smiled wide, the grin illuminating his face and highlighting the laugh lines and small wrinkles around his eyes. "Then consider this detour my peace offering."

"Really?"

"That and my way of preventing you from sneaking off in the middle of the night, which is what you would have probably done if I'd acted like the overbearing bodyguard."

Sophia chuckled under her breath because Teija knew her too well. "You know with the position of the sun, if we stop, we may not be able to get back on the road in time to make it to the territory marker."

"Don't say I never did anything for you."

They both went silent, though she appreciated her friend's kindness. He didn't have to be, even though she'd decided to go to Frog Lick the moment she saw the shiny metal buildings reflecting light from the sun. And once Sophia Archer decided to do something, she'd guarantee it happened, no matter what.

Chapter Three

Sophia took a deep breath and tried to calm her galloping heart, a combination of nerves and being yanked out of an open doorway. Teija stood behind her, tying Sophia's head cover into the rings on her jacket collar.

"You need to hide yourself," he'd said as he pulled her out of the Watering Hole entrance, his worry stemming from the potential of others recognizing her.

But then, the very person she'd been seeking had walked out of the door. All six-foot tall, creamy clay-colored skin with dark curly hair and golden eyes she could drown in. Like a sea of melted crinkle. He was glorious, though now half of him was metal. She saw the shine on his neck, his left forearm, hand and fingers. *How much of him is like this?*

"Sophia."

Teija huffed behind her, and she imagined him rolling his eyes. He had an awkward sense of belief that she should be formally addressed like she was in their gang-town of Aurestral. She didn't care whether they added a "Lady" or not. The silly rules of their gang, and the surrounding ones in gangs throughout Aurora, were a bit more patriarchal than she cared for.

"Hemi." This time she wasn't saying it out of shock or wonder, but with the relief of knowing he lived. He wasn't a figment of her daydreams or worries any longer. "I'm so happy to see you."

Hemi cleared his throat. "Funny running into you here. What brings you to Frog Lick?"

"Would you believe me if I said you?"

"Don't play coy, do you?" Teija whispered to her.

She'd lost enjoyment in such games, especially with the future barreling down on her. This was her one shot to do something for herself amid the expectations of her family. Once the sun rose the next morning, she'd have to say goodbye to her momentary freedom and commit to the future laid out by her parents. So, screw the shy, shallow games of conversation. For a single moment in time, she wanted to be as honest as possible.

"I'm surprised. Figured after our last chat, your plans weren't going to involve being anywhere near me."

Sure, she'd said a few things and tried to get Hemi to give her any inclination he felt anything for her and nothing had happened. She'd crushed on him since the moment they'd met, hard. Her mission from the second she'd run into him trying to get out of her studies for the day had involved keeping his attention. She'd been knocked stupid, as her mother would say. His eyes…she couldn't breathe when looking into them. He'd shown her parts of Aurestral she'd never seen, the underbelly of a gang-town that had serious disparity, and her goal had morphed into trying to save him from a life of debt.

Except he was supposed to be hers after she did the saving. Instead, he'd quit Aurestral and gone an entire region away.

"Figured I'd give you one last chance."

"To what?"

"Convince me why I shouldn't agree to an arranged marriage."

Hemi rubbed his jaw, and she recognized the simple tell. She'd shocked him, and she grinned in response.

"I think this conversation might be easier to understand if we had a couple drinks to go with it."

"You can't go in there," Teija whispered, attempting to act as her good sense, but she'd decided to ditch good sense as soon as Teija had agreed to let her detour to Frog Lick.

"Why not?"

"Someone may recognize—"

"She'll keep the hood up, and I'll protect her. No one will dare to approach if she's with me." Hemi's words sent a flutter of warm feelings all through her chest at the idea of him offering to watch over her.

Teija let out a low growl. "Are you sure you're capable in such an injured state?"

"We can put things to the test here or keep everything friendly and let me enjoy a drink with an old friend on her last adventure of freedom."

Friend? I don't want to be a friend.

She'd wanted to be far more, mean more. Though she'd settle for the moment and keep her spirits high with the knowledge that Hemi was willing to offer her protection to enjoy herself.

Teija sighed beside her. "This is what you want?"

"Yes," she replied without hesitation.

"Then I'll retrieve you in the morning." Teija walked away along with the driver to who knew where, and for the moment, she didn't care.

"Lead the way then, Hemi."

Hemi gave a weak smile that didn't quite reach his eyes, and motioned toward the Watering Hole door. Sophia followed, doing her best to keep her strut contained and her scarf in place. She wanted to loop her arm through his and give him a playful squeeze. Her desire to be close warred with the good sense to keep her distance.

You haven't seen him in months and before that... He'd disappeared into the night. Off to seek a future without her. They crossed the threshold into the bar, and Sophia was immediately immersed in a foreign world. From the harmonizing strums of the guitar, the hum of conversations, the clink of mugs of ale and the scents of hops, barley and spice, she longed for another week to experience everything this place had to offer.

Hemi moved toward the nearest table, in a corner of the room, not far from the door. He pulled out a chair and waved her over. When she sat down, he leaned in and spoke directly into her ear. "I'll get us a couple ales and a bowl of stew with dumplings, if you're hungry?"

That low baritone of his voice flooded her body with arousal. Funny how he'd always turned her on, and she'd had embarrassingly little to show for her severe attraction. Unable to speak for a moment, she nodded her head. As Hemi moved away, she clenched her fists. *Get a hold of yourself.*

She'd gone from merely wanting to know if he was alive to losing her damn shit just from him talking to her. Of course, add in the fact he pulled out her chair... Even with the cybernetic surgery, he was still Hemi. *Still ridiculously gorgeous.*

"Here we go." Hemi slid two mugs onto the table then took a seat across from her. "Food should be over shortly."

She reached for the mug, merely to occupy her hands, and gripped it tight between both palms. "How much do I owe you?"

"Nothing. That's not how things work here." He took a long swallow and she couldn't help but notice the metal on the left side of his neck. The contrast to its solid, unmoving state compared to the creamy brown skin on his right side.

She took a drink herself, to clear the dry path in her throat. *Beyond thirsty.* "Strange, I thought every territory charged for food and drink. Isn't it criminal not to?"

"Drag, our leader, doesn't believe that way. He figures it's kindness to give folks at least ale and food when they pass through. Doing right by people is what got me to stay in Frog Lick in the first place. Full Throttle has some strange ideas, but so far they've created a gang-town with far more potential than I've seen anywhere else. Here anyone can be who they want to be."

The words had chill bumps breaking out over her arms. The final musical notes of the latest song paired with those ideas sparked riotous thoughts in her mind. How she longed to chase her own dreams, to be the person in charge of Aurestral, to choose whether she wanted to marry or not.

"I can see how that would be tempting. What else made you decide to stay? Looks like there are plenty of attractive dust honeys as well." She laid her traps the same way gang scavengers trapped goosemert or fur-buns. A spark of jealousy ignited in anticipation toward whatever woman snared Hemi's bed or heart.

He chuckled low. "Yes, there is that, but my focus has been on racing. Sure, a dust honey or two can pass a lonely night, but that's not the long haul. Winning races is. I stayed to drive and Drag gave me that opportunity."

There was a lot there unsaid, and she didn't want this night to be soured by more bad memories.

"So, you came to Frog Lick to see me, for a chat?" The question came with another half-grin. Hemi didn't appear to want to dwell in the past either. Instead, he'd make it harder on her in the present.

How desperate do I want to appear? How silly?

"I was on my way to Auster, and my future."

"Husband?"

"Fiancé." She took another swallow, hoping the liquid gave her courage. Except she ended up downing it. When she set the mug back down, a woman with keen blue eyes and a long, pale-blonde braid hanging halfway down her back slid a bowl onto the table.

"There's the stew. Looks like you need an ale refill."

"That and something a little stronger, Gaia," Hemi added and handed off his mug as well.

Gaia nodded. "Be right back."

Something stronger…maybe my news had an effect.

"The arrangements have been made and I…"

"Deserve a drink to celebrate the upcoming nuptials. Last night of freedom, I get it. What better way to spend the time than with a friend? Eat up." Hemi glanced around them, eyes anywhere but on her.

Sophia did her best not to frown and picked the spoon out of the bowl. The stew with dumplings, whatever those were, smelled delicious and she scooped some into her mouth. Savory broth, with spice and warmth, along with flavor that reminded her of roasted fur bun burst over her tongue.

Her stomach rumbled in response and she shoveled the food into her mouth as quickly as she could.

"Hey, slow down a bit."

"This is amazing," she replied in between bites.

"I know. It's my specialty." Gaia set down a pair of smaller glasses, a dark bottle and two filled mugs of ale. "Enjoy yourself and let me know if you need another bowl. Everyone is welcome to at least two."

Then the woman was away, weaving through the tables and off to provide service to others.

"Is everyone so nice here too?"

Hemi spun the top off the bottle and started pouring. "Unless you give them a reason not to be."

He slid a full glass over to her, the amber liquid sloshing over the sides onto the table.

"What's that?" she asked as she finished off the last of the stew, and the last bite of a wet biscuit-like dumpling.

"Whiskey. The good stuff. Only way to celebrate an impending wedding."

She picked up the glass, recalling when her father would share a little sip with her after a negotiations celebration or when he'd secured something for the gang. Her memories were also filled with the reminder that whiskey burned. *Why does anyone enjoy drinking this stuff?* "Any trick to this?"

"Don't breathe. Down it and then exhale. Doesn't burn as much." Hemi lifted his glass. "To your marriage."

Sophia lifted hers and clicked the glass against his. Then she threw it back. The burn was there, but not as bad, and she let out a slow exhale as he'd suggested. The amber liquid pooled in her belly, spreading warmth throughout and a slight tingle.

Hemi held the bottle up, a single eyebrow raised.

"Another."

* * * *

The bottle was almost gone, with at least a half inch left inside, and Sophia couldn't keep her mouth shut. *Whiskey draws all the words out.*

"I don't want to, Hemi. I'm not ready to marry and especially not to someone I don't even know. Besides, I'd always hoped I could take over the gang in Aurestral myself. My spouse would defer to me, not the other way around. These are the days I wish I'd been born male."

Hemi nodded in agreement, reaching out across the table with his human hand. He traced the tips of her fingers and she almost moaned as he encased her hand in his. The warmth, the calluses, his touch in general had always inspired foolish thoughts.

"I get it. You've wanted to be in charge since day one."

She winked at him. "In every aspect of my life."

She giggled and let herself bask in this unguarded moment. Though she needed to get a hold of herself.

"What can I do though? If I don't show up in Osprerine without a good reason, it will cause problems. But I truly believe I need time to come up with another solution that doesn't involve me tying myself to someone who won't care for Aurestral like I would." She started to pull away from him, hating how needy her voice sounded, how holding onto him only reminded her of what she'd never have.

He tightened his grip, and she stilled, staring into those golden eyes that were intently focused on her. She licked her lips and he matched her actions.

"I get what you're saying and I have an idea. If you're willing."

Willing… She was desperate.

Chapter Four

Hemi woke with a start, sitting straight up in bed, head pounding and desperate for water.

Water... He glanced at the table beside the bed and reached for the closed container of recycle he kept there. That was one thing the remaining human parts of him needed — water. The other Full Throttle members never had that much of a problem, since they'd only had one appendage each replaced. With half of his body cybernetic, Hemi's body heat naturally ran hotter than most, causing him to dehydrate faster.

He took a long swallow and sighed in relief as the cool liquid hit his throat and lower, though the pain in his head still lingered.

What happened last night?

A low female moan came from beside him, and Hemi froze. He'd said no to Josie and Haimea. He remembered that much, and even walking out of the Watering Hole. *What happened next?*

Another moan, and the shifting of weight on the bed... a female hand, tan skin, slender fingers falling over his forearm. He dared a glance and saw wavy blonde hair spread across a fully clothed body.

Thank the spirits. Sophia.

The memories hit him like a racer plowing into a retainer wall. She'd shown up, they'd shared a drink, she'd eaten then more drinks. Lots of drinks, because fuck... *She's getting married.*

He'd been determined to play things cool, detached. Then more drinks. *The entire fucking bottle of whiskey.* The Watering Hole near closing, yet Privy had kept on playing his guitar. When Sophia had finally confessed she didn't want to marry, he'd been relieved, but then foolish enough to offer an idea so ridiculous...

"No," he whispered. He turned his arm over, Sophia's fingers still loosely draped against him, and there was the pick and hammer tattoo right under his Full Throttle brand.

He glanced at her hand on him. Her jacket long gone, she wore only a short-sleeved faded yellow shirt. Reaching for her wrist, he carefully turned over her left arm, and found a tattoo that matched his.

"Holy shit." He jumped out of the bed to a standing position and scrubbed his face with both hands. Then he almost lost his balance and snatched up his cane that was leaning against the wall next to the bed, which prevented him from making an even bigger fool of himself. The temptation to smack himself awake from this dream world was all too tempting.

The woman was sprawled across the left side of the bed, face down, ass up, and... *What a damn delectable ass.* Two perfectly round globes clad in form-fitting pants. Her shirt had risen a bit from movement and her midriff was visible...soft skin, a little roll. That blonde hair in waves…and she'd propped her head up on one hand to look at him.

Her smile made it evident she'd caught him admiring her. "Good morning."

"I don't know if it's good. Seems we might have got up to some mischief last night."

"Can't say I didn't enjoy it if we did."

"Your arm." He pointed at the tattoo, the one meaning they were bonded together…married.

"It was your idea."

Hemi scrubbed his face again, trying to wipe away the loss of memory and the confusion. Had he really suggested they get married? The recall was slow, but there. She'd been desperate, so beautiful and heartbroken at being sent to marry a man she didn't know.

That much he'd gleaned from her pouting lips, those blue eyes the color of a Neptunian sea haunting him. The tears had gathered in the corners, threatening to track a path down her cheeks, and she'd let out a little hiccup. He remembered that perfectly.

The moment of her vulnerability was at odds with everything he'd ever seen from Sophia. She'd been strong, proud and louder than anyone he'd ever met. Her plea and desire for a future she could control spoke to his own fierce need for independence. Nevertheless, her confession about her circumstances and wish for time to figure her own path had sent him down a reckless one.

"I agreed to help you."

Help, not fuck. But those sun-kissed locks of hers, the cool sandy color of her skin…he wanted to figure out if she was as soft as she'd been when they kissed last night. When Privy had married them on the damn stage and Gaia had acted as witness along with Rune... *Fuck, Drag's brother.* The whole town would know by now and he wouldn't escape the questions. Rune had been the one to watch as Privy completed the tattoos. The Watering Hole guitarist had hidden depths.

"And I'm grateful, Hemi." Sophia pushed up onto all fours and crawled across the bed toward him. Even fully clothed, she was still a temptation, made all the worse by how her shirt hung loose in the middle and he had a good view of her tits from this angle. Rounded mounds of luscious flesh...he licked his lips.

No. That's not what this is.

"It's no big deal." Was his back against the wall? The solid surface was cool against half of him, and the other half was dead to any sense. That was what he needed to remember—he was only half the man he used to be. For her he could only be this support system, nothing more and nothing less. Anything else would just end in disappointment for her. Especially if Jack and Shannon didn't succeed.

Jack...

"But it is." She was perched on her legs now, knees bent. "You didn't have to do this for me at all. I wouldn't be surprised if Teija pitches a fit—"

"Do I need to say something?"

She smiled. "You would, but no. I'll handle him and I promise I won't make this marriage last any longer than I need to."

Hemi was still plastered against the wall, trying to decide if he would be an ass for asking how much time she needed. *No, be calm and give her a chance to adjust.* Forcing himself away from the wall, he approached her. Keeping his back straight allowed him to ignore the pain in his human leg as he shifted his weight to the cane.

"You're figuring out a future for you and Aurestral, and if I know anything from Drag's stories of taking over Frog Lick and this gang, answers take time."

Her grin widened and he tried not to get too excited, knowing he'd said the right thing. She'd been at the top for too long with people who would only ever pander to her or insult her into silence. He'd seen those actions firsthand, and he could be the opposite. Instead of a voice of insult, a listening ear, an encourager, at least until he decided if his own future lay with Full Throttle or somewhere else. *Because it sure as hell doesn't belong in a driver's seat.*

"How is it you always know what to say? First last night, and now."

He shrugged. "Natural talent?" *Or just speaking what I would want someone to say to me.*

The something missing in his own life was what he could give to her. In ways Full Throttle had become those voices of support, until they'd unilaterally decided to swap half his body for cybernetics.

"Well, you certainly weren't this good ten years ago."

"I was a kid then, now I'm a man." He froze as her eyes trailed over him from the waist up. She didn't look at him like he was disgusting, even though the cybernetic part of him was more on display since he wore a simple tank and shorts. He'd been so caught up in the situation, he hadn't thought to throw on more clothes.

Sophia licked her lips as her gaze finally settled on his. "I noticed."

"Still a flirt." He reached out and ruffled her hair, setting his hand against her scalp and confirming her hair was indeed as soft as he'd imagined.

She dodged away from him and frowned. "Don't dismiss my actions like I'm not aware of what I'm doing. At least let me repay your help in some way."

"Not that way." *Hell no.* He wasn't even sure about engaging in physical activity with anyone. He could hurt her. "You can keep your pants on and your libido tucked away. That's not what I was revving for when I made my offer."

Liar.

"You needed a place to gather your thoughts without someone pressuring you to the altar. If we're married, that solves the problem. I'm a genius." *More like an idiot.* Because he couldn't stand how disappointed she looked. He'd been turning her down for half his life and he wasn't going to give in now. She'd needed to accept the fact they weren't meant to be anything more than friends because he didn't belong where she did. Though the insidious reminder of how her father had claimed Hemi would never marry his daughter had been proven wrong and a small bit of the rebel inside him preened.

"I get it. You don't want to fall for me." Her smirk came with a flash of that fire she'd always carried. Her eyes ignited like a spark of lightning right before a storm. She was damn dangerous to a man's ego and his thought process.

"Princess, I'm nothing worth chasing. You're just used to everyone giving you what you want, and hate being told no. I'm not one of your fuck boys, ready for you to use and discard. I don't think you'd appreciate me too much if I was."

She pouted. "You're just like Teija."

"No, we're nothing alike because Teija's engines get revved up for a different team. I'll pedal to the metal for the ladies, but in your case, I think I enjoy telling you no more."

The way she fisted the sheet from his bed and kicked her feet against the mattress was adorable. This he could handle, their back and forth, tossing off her deliberate, playful attempts to get him to see her as something much more. The only problem was he'd always seen her as a woman, a damn attractive one that he'd love to have in many carnal ways. Except he was broken now.

That fact had been made clear to him the day he left Aurestral and struck out to find his own path. There would be no happy-ever-after. No marrying the princess and being the boy who'd risen from the dust and the dirt to castle life. The least he could do was play the knight who'd defend her against all comers.

A knock on his front door stopped all of Sophia's movements.

The sun was up, the morning bell probably minutes away from ringing. Hemi motioned to Sophia. "Stay here."

"But—"

"Stay." Because no way did he want to have any conversations about Sophia with the other members of Full Throttle. *Not yet*. He marched into the main room and over to the door, cracking it open to avoid a full assault from the morning sun since his porch faced east.

The looming shape in front of him could only belong to one man.

"Drag, what brings you over before the bell?"

"We need to talk. Now." No frown, no frustration in his voice, just an emotionless command. At least Drag wasn't acting like he was upset about Hemi's change in relationship status or issuing ultimatums.

Hemi couldn't help but glance over his shoulder. The relief at not seeing Sophia in the main room was almost like the pure joy of an ion shower taking away the grime of the day. "Does it have to happen right this second or can I—"

"Meet me at the shop when you're ready. Preferably soon-ish. It's not about the wedding. It's about Jack."

Jack…his friend, mentor and the guy willing to sacrifice himself as a guinea pig to stop the nanites controlling their cybernetic components from killing them. To say he'd let Sophia distract him was a damn understatement.

"I'll be there in a bit."

Drag nodded, then walked off. Hemi shut the door then leaned against it, resting his head against his arm. He hadn't missed Drag mentioning the wedding. Word had already spread across Full Throttle. There were no secrets in this place.

Yet while he'd offered Sophia time and space, he seemed to have forgotten the most important thing was that he needed to focus on getting himself in tip-top shape because soon he'd have to make decisions on whether he stayed in Frog Lick.

"Hemi?" Sophia's voice, like a siren's song of sultry tones, called his name. She had to be at the entrance to the room. Her soft footsteps approached him. He couldn't help but shiver as her fingertips touched his shoulder. When was the last time someone had touched him in a caring way?

"Is everything okay?" she whispered.

He dared to lift his head a bit, his gaze colliding with her sea-blue eyes.

No, nothing will ever be okay again.

Chapter Five

Sophia wanted to wrap Hemi up in her arms, hold him close and never let go. She could tell from his gaze that his thoughts were tumbling in so many directions. When he'd offered to marry her last night, she had selfishly said yes. For the chance he'd given her to find her own way without having to sacrifice her gang and who she was to a person she didn't know.

Of course, when the man offering was the one she'd dreamed about marrying since she was ten years old, it was difficult to say no even when she knew he wouldn't make it a reality. Except that kiss... *No time to think about it now.*

"You can talk to me."

He'd been a listening ear for her, a support. She could return the favor. She dared to spread her hand wide and caress his shoulder, his body heat a reminder that, regardless of the half-cybernetic part, he was still human.

Except he pulled away, stepping back from her. "Everything is fine. There's some Full Throttle business I need to attend to in the mechanics bay. So, I'll be gone most of the day, but that bonding tattoo will get you just about anything you need. Food, water, extra clothing."

Here she was trying to get closer, and he widened the gap between them. "It's a little hard to do all of that exploring on my own."

He gave her that little-half smile with his cocked eyebrow. "And you've never shied away from a chance at an adventure in your life. Don't start pretending you're afraid to be on your own now."

"But…" She flicked her fingers against her thumbs, trying to come up with a reason that wasn't the truth. "I don't know these people."

"Gaia fed you two bowls of her stew and dumplings with a bottle of whiskey and didn't care. Trust me, you won't find a more welcoming place than here in Frog Lick. We get passers-through, new prospects and wanderers all the time. Are you worried about Teija?"

She blew air out through her lips. "No, he'll do what he needs to, and I'll stick to my guns. Besides, you and I both know I do what I want."

"Truer words. That's the strong, independent Sophia I know. Take this chance to have your space. No commitments, no expectations, just you figuring out what your future holds and how you can mold it in a way that meets what you want."

His words sent a slither of hope through her. She was wild, fierce, brave…all those things and she damn well knew it. The fact Hemi did too made her love him all the more. Fool she was, loving him when all he tried to do was be a friend to her.

"Then I'll take that challenge and try to figure things out on my own while you take care of your business. But don't be a stranger."

He winked at her. "Of course not. We're sharing a house, but I'll take the couch tonight."

Said couch was threadbare, barely more than a couple stuffed cushions wrapped around some planks. It would be uncomfortable as hell from the looks of it, and Hemi probably needed more support with his new body.

"No, if it's that important to you that we sleep separate, I can take the couch. You need to be on something softer and bigger than that old thing."

"Hey!" Hemi let out a chuckle amid his mock outrage. "I helped build that myself. Even picked the fabric cover. It's got style and love that should bring comfort enough."

If only those things did. If she could simply voice her love to get a similar reaction from him, one filled with more than friendly affection… She craved desire, the same look that she had believed passed his face when she'd crawled across the bed toward him a little bit ago.

He'd looked at her then, and she couldn't help but imagine closing the distance, easily remembering the way he'd kissed her last night at the conclusion of the ceremony, at Gaia and Rune's urging. He'd placed his hands on her, one hot, one cold then his lips. She recalled the soft, tentative touch that had felt like a dream, only for it to turn hot and molten like Marsanium ore when melted. She'd moaned, then tongues were involved.

Fuck. She was wet all over again and she licked her lips.

For a split second she could have sworn Hemi's gaze reflected a hunger that rivaled her own. Instead, he clapped his hands and sighed. "All right then. I'm getting dressed and I'll let you hunt down Teija to give him the bad news."

"Huh?"

"That you're married to the one man your father said could never have you."

She stood there slack-jawed as Hemi turned away, marched into the bedroom then slammed the door behind him.

What the hell did I miss? And when did he ask if he could have me?

Sophia wanted to demand answers but opted for a visit to the facilities. She ran her fingers through her hair and became determined to ferret out the truth behind Hemi's statement one way or another. For now she had another beast to quell—her bodyguard.

Teija.

She sighed. This wouldn't be easy. He'd agreed to her little detour with the expectation she would toe her father's decree in return. Not that she would full-on rebel like a child throwing a tantrum for not getting a treat.

Of course, she would have gone along with things if Hemi hadn't offered her this solution. Though if what Hemi had said was true, did Teija know something about this as well? *Stupid.*

She slapped her cheeks gently, then harder in a bid to come back to reality. Love and being with a man she'd always wanted needed to take a back seat to the bigger issues. Her good arguments.

And... *I need to find the jerk first.* Teija would probably be where food was. Hemi's place wasn't far from the Watering Hole and Sophia was thankful for the sun goggles she'd found hanging by the door. She needed all the protection she could get because the walkways and streets weren't shrouded like they were in Aurestral. No, unlike the thin tapestries that hung between buildings to filter out the sunlight and offer a semblance of protection to gang members, in Wespero, the gangs lived in the wide-open space.

Sunlight beat down upon the red earth with sparse plant life, reflecting off metal roofs and other building surfaces. In general, an annoyance she'd have to deal with since she'd made her decision last night. She tugged at the edges of her head scarf, ensuring it was in place. Better to have something to appease Teija, even the tiniest bit.

She was married. A smile bloomed on her lips and she couldn't help but let happiness spread through her as she pushed through the Watering Hole's entrance. Sure enough, her target was sitting on a bar stool shoveling food from a bowl into his mouth.

She slipped onto the seat next to him and sighed. "You're so predictable. I could have guessed where you were straight away."

"Really? Whereas you break promises and make me for a fool time and again. One would think I'd learn the lesson, but it appears not."

Okay, that hurts. She was briefly reminded of the number of times she'd slipped away from Teija. The times she had him cover for her while she'd run off to see a practice race or to hear stories in Aurestral's square. She'd always come back, but not without somehow breaking her agreement with Teija.

"It was a few minutes late with the races, and the storyteller asked for a volunteer. Those other times I was helping our people, and how was I to know that my father told Hemi to never court me?"

The last part of the sentence caught Teija's attention. His hand froze, spoon suspended. He quickly recovered, shoveling another mouthful of his breakfast past his lips.

"So, you're not going to deny it." She needed to know. It was as important as coming here to see Hemi one last time. Would all her efforts to try to win him be ruined by her father's meddling?

"Why do you act surprised? Your father has always actively spoken with those who might bring more trouble than help when it comes to you." Teija kept eating, his gaze focused forward, his long brown hair with gold tufts here and there pulled back into a low ponytail. His ears were pierced multiple times with various pins and pieces of shiny gems lining the shell. She'd always thought him brave and an ally, but now...

"You could have told me years ago, before he left."

"It would only have made you rebel even harder, though it appears you still haven't grown up. Selfish as always." He pushed the bowl away with a sigh. "You've always done whatever you wanted, no thought to consequences, and I would back you, but I can't this time. You think you're the only one being forced to give up what they want?"

Teija looked at her then. Those dark brown eyes of his were filled with pain, disappointment and a reminder of all the ways their world stopped them from being who they were.

"So, you're saying you're okay with everything as long as I suffer with you?" She clenched her fists and tapped them against the bar top. "Why live in a world of punishment when I can have what I want?"

Her question came out low, with a snarl.

"You could have tried for both, duty and happiness." There were a lot of things left unsaid there. Teija wanted her hiding in the shadows, like those who chased goosemerts at dusk. Getting only a sliver of joy, when she believed she could find a way to have it all.

"I refuse, Teija. Maybe you're right — it was a fool's bargain to agree to my plan to come here and now Aurestral's future may be in question, but I won't turn down this chance."

As their conversation continued, the bar itself filled with the constant din of discussion and people coming and going. Sophia didn't miss the fact Gaia had yet to ask her if she wanted a drink or food. The pale-blonde barkeep with her almost ethereal figure and boisterous mouth stayed at opposite ends or out on the floor, leaving Teija and Sophia to mostly communicate between themselves.

Of course, they couldn't say outright what they felt. Even in their younger years Teija and Sophia had coded dialogues because otherwise trouble would follow. Except she longed to speak plainly with him, desired a future where they didn't need to hide who they were.

"You do what you think you have to, Teija. I'll do the same. But this isn't just about me, no matter how selfish you think I am."

Sure, her desire for Hemi could easily consume her. From his smiles, to his body, to the way he handled a racer and even to his ability to make her think in different ways. She could get lost in his eyes, corrupted by his hands or devoured by his lips. *Damn those lips.*

But no…she gave her head a little shake. "I'll show you it's about a future we both can have happiness in."

"You'll never convince him, and when I report this, they will come for you." Teija twisted in his seat to face her. She could see the remorse there, but he was duty bound and would suffer for letting her marry someone besides her betrothed.

"If that's what happens, then they come. But I'm going to use every spare minute searching for a solution that gets everyone what they want."

"Living in old Earth tales."

She grinned at him. "Not then, but the now. We can weave a future we want. Just look at Full Throttle. If they can do this, so can I."

"Maybe, but are you willing to risk Aurestral on such a gamble?"

Chapter Six

Sophia stayed on her stool for a good ten minutes after Teija left, staring at the wall in front of her. The wooden shelf contained glasses, bowls and mugs of multiple shapes and sizes. There were bottles side-by-side below holding various colored liquids, ranging from clear to near black. The contents inside were a mystery.

Had Teija been right? Was she risking everything for her own happiness and selfishly caring only about herself?

A tall glass of clear liquid appeared in front of her and Sophia blinked before glancing up at Gaia.

"Looks like you need something refreshing. Take a sip of that."

Sophia shook her head. "It's too early for liquor."

"I know, and exactly why I didn't serve you booze. Trust me, this will hit the spot." The woman winked at her then left to tend to another customer who'd called her name.

Sophia grabbed the glass and sniffed — nothing was what she smelled in return. A strange sensation to get nothing off a beverage. She took a long swallow and her other hand slapped against the bar top hard.

Water, crisp, clean and fresher than anything she'd ever tasted slid down her throat. She couldn't help herself but to take two more good hard swallows, relishing in the cool liquid that typically held mud and iron tastes, or the faint odor and color of residue left from reuse. Recycle was the most common, water processed for safe consumption. Yet no process any gang possessed could get water this clean on Mars. No, only the Uppers had that type of technology.

She set the glass down and stared at it in wonder. *How did they do this?*

The bar had quieted and Sophia noticed there weren't too many folks inside. She should have gotten going, done something at Hemi's or figured out dinner. Instead, she was sitting here wondering where to go, then this water had appeared.

"You've got the same look anyone who gets a good drink always has. Made you feel better, right?" Gaia asked, coming to a half in front of her. "Don't let it sit too long. Tastes better when it's freshly poured. Cooler, too."

"It's refreshing and unlike anything I've had before. How?"

Gaia waved a finger at her. "Now, now. I don't tell gang secrets. Think of this as a wedding gift to you. I'll also be willing to give you a tour of Frog Lick so you know where things are. Not today, mind you. It's a busy day, the beginning of our week, prepping our menu and ensuring we have the supplies to care for all."

"Sounds like a lot of work." Sophia had known of many who worked hard in Aurestral, but all for the purpose of putting themselves ahead. A more capitalist society, as her father referred to the way business worked. *Let the people drive their future.* Though she saw more hunger, more greed and desperation at home. Her father led through mediation and ensuring the overall benefit of the gang, but steered clear of daily involvement.

"It is, but here we support the community as a whole. When bellies are full and people aren't dying of thirst, they become a lot more productive."

"What of those who want to care for themselves?"

Gaia grinned. "They are more than welcome to. Though we still give them supplies to do so. They don't have to share a meal here. All they are asked to do is hold a productive role with the town."

"No other option is provided." Sophia finished off the water, holding the glass back to let the last drop fall on her lips. "Seems a bit too easy. Not everyone can work, not everyone has skills."

"You'd think that, but that's not true. They do. Even someone who can only sit on a stool can wash things. Those missing a limb can still teach others to read, to build ships. We provide free medical care here, too. Maybe that's what you're not used to. Seeing folks being cared for."

Not in the way Gaia described it, no, but the barkeep's passionate words clearly told Sophia she was in the right place because this was what she dreamed of for Aurestral. Less fighting and bickering for resources, less illness, fewer discarded folk and more mutual beneficial interaction.

"You treat the town and the gang like a true symbiosis. Everyone working in tandem to support a function."

"Those are fancy words, but yes. Seems like you got yourself an education somewhere. A Mars bred and raised talking like an Upper. Good thing you married straight away."

Sophia chuckled. "Why?"

"Because not everyone who passes through is a good sort, and such a valuable prize, pretty, well-mannered and can speak fancy will get you plucked and sold off-world in a heartbeat."

Seemed traffickers were everywhere. "Nothing changes. Thanks for the drink."

"Sure, and don't let what your friend said bother you. You're not selfish for wanting a better future. Everyone here felt the same way, wanted more. We were willing to back a leader that would give us the opportunity to pursue this life. Can't blame others for recognizing its value. You're safe here."

Gaia left, disappearing behind the bar into another room. A door tottered shut and a lock slid in place. A couple folks still mingled either in a booth or at a table, but they were busy with their own conversations. Whatever was happening, it appeared the folks of Frog Lick were busy as Gaia said, pursuing their own duties. Sophia needed to figure out what hers would be. Though, she'd start with Hemi's house. Teija had said he'd leave her things there, so she needed to set herself up. With Hemi unwilling to sleep with her, for now, she'd need to get a bed together.

There was plenty to do and think about. It sucked she'd have to do it alone until Hemi was finished with work. Because if there was one person who could help guide her now, it would be him.

* * * *

"Married? I can't fucking believe it." Snapper's voice echoed across the mechanics bay. If anyone didn't know, they did now. "Who the hell would marry you?"

"Gaia called her a great beauty." Gina said this without pulling her head from the beneath the hood of the racer she was tweaking, a new prototype Jack had been putting through its paces only days prior.

"You said this was about Jack."

"I lied." Drag stood against a far wall, arms crossed with the cybernetic one gleaming in the light filtering through the skylights. He and Snapper were like twins with matching opposing arms and shoulders. Though that was where the similarities ended. Drag was all sun-kissed skin and light-blond hair with a clean-shaven face, whereas Snapper was dark, with cheeks and chin that always had a good coat of hair.

Hemi often wondered how he maintained the look without becoming a bushman, but instead he found himself annoyed today. "Why?"

"What's your plan with the Aurestral princess?"

Fuck. Drag even knew who she was. "How did you know—"

"Because her bodyguard was beating down my door this morning demanding I invalidate the marriage. She was promised to another, the son of the Osprerine leader. Is it worth reminding you we already have axes to grind with the Macintosh bastards for what they did to you? Full Throttle doesn't need to be dragged into territory disputes."

Hemi was an idiot, of that he was aware, but—"She's not territory, she's a person. Isn't that what you're always talking about, Drag? People should be free to choose. Her parents are forcing this arrangement on her, and she doesn't even know the man."

"Did she ask for your help?"

Not directly, no. Sophia would have never put him in that situation, except he knew her. Had known her for more than half his life. She came running to him whenever she had a problem no one else would listen to. She'd sought him out for a listening ear and an escape nearly every day from the moment they'd met on one of her ill-fated adventures into the Aurestral square.

"Even if she hadn't, I still would give it. She's the reason I'm even a racer. If it wasn't for her, you wouldn't have a championship bid." He'd play that excuse as many times as he needed to. He left out the part where they'd fucked up his body without his permission…yet, if he'd died on that racing track, he wouldn't have been here to help Sophia.

"They will come for her." Snapper's voice was low and deep, the words spoken in such a way that hit Hemi square in the chest.

He struggled against that errant emotion, one he'd fought many times in the years since Sophia's father had spoken his decree. "I know and that's fine. When they do, I won't hesitate to let her go. I'm just giving her time. She wants to be the one to lead her gang. Not turn everything over to someone else, but she needs time to figure out how to do that. I…"

Drag cleared his throat and looked at him, one eyebrow raised in question.

"We," Hemi amended. "Can do that for her. Show her what life is like here, give her information, knowledge for how gang life could be."

"Yes, but that doesn't change years and years of repressed thinking based on antiquated ideals meant to keep others oppressed. Even you, who came to us, had difficulty adjusting at first to how we did things. It won't be easy." Drag pushed off the wall and came toward him. It was a few heavy steps, then that cybernetic hand was on Hemi's matching shoulder. "But if you think she's worth the time and the effort? Fine."

Did he though? *Yes, of course...* He ignored the twinge in his chest, that yearning for something more, and focused on the root of why he'd offered this option to her to begin with. She wanted to create a future for Aurestral like Full Throttle had. One where people who fell for those not their equal or from a different class didn't have to give up love or what they truly wanted. *Where anyone can be anyone.*

Drag and the others could show her how to make it possible. Hemi was just the person who could give her a moment's peace to see it.

"She is. I believe she wants to spread the same type of equality we have here to Aurestral. What better way to learn how to do so than being exposed to the very heart of what you created, Drag?"

The smile Drag gave Hemi was so genuine, with admiration and thankfulness in his eyes as if Hemi truly understood what Drag had pursued since taking over. Though Hemi couldn't return it because he still resented what they'd done to him...saving him and creating a monster in its place.

"Then good. I think we'll all be happy to help. For now, I need your eyes on this engine with Gina. If Jack doesn't come back, you're our best hope. I don't mean to take you away from your physical therapy or even Sophia, but—"

"It's fine. All hands, right? I'm the racer, that's what I signed up for." Hemi stepped out of Drag's hold and marched over to Gina's side. "Tell me what you need me to do."

Until he made his final decision, Hemi would keep working alongside the people who saved his life. He'd find a way.

Chapter Seven

Hemi helped until he was too exhausted to move. Snapper was setting him up on the couch the head engineer kept in his office.

"You should go home." Snapper tossed him a blanket and moved Hemi's cane to rest against a chair, but still within reach.

"I can barely walk. I pushed too hard today. I fell trying to help lift that engine block."

"You're an idiot. Doesn't mean I can't carry you." Snapper's words were matter-of-fact. The man towered over him as he lay on the couch. "Say the word and I'll get you to your own bed, which is going to be far more comfortable than this scratchy fabric and thin-ass cushioning."

"No." Hemi shook his head. "Leave me here for the night. Don't want Sophia to worry. Tell her we have too much happening."

"Are you sure you want to stay married to this woman? I mean, most men can't wait to be with their spouse. There are perks to them worrying over you."

It was on the tip of Hemi's tongue to tell Snapper the truth. That he hadn't attempted to have sex with anyone since the accident. There were plenty of offers, but he was too afraid and fucking Sophia... *Too tempting*. Because he'd swore to give her up. He'd walked away determined never to give into physical temptation, yet he'd married her at the first available option.

"There are, but that's not what this marriage is about."

Snapper chuckled. "Sure, buddy. Keep telling yourself that, but Rune was there when you two kissed at the ceremony. From his perspective, there were plenty of emotions being displayed in that kiss."

"Just because you have them doesn't mean you act on them." Hemi had felt some strong things for Shannon too and kept his distance. Maybe he enjoyed punishing himself as well, but he might not recover from this cybernetic transplant, at least never completely. *Why put someone else through that?*

"Leave me here. I'll help some more when I get up."

Snapper shook out the threadbare blanket and spread it over him. "Fine, whatever you want. Don't complain about the noise, though. Since the explosion, Gina doesn't want to sleep at my place. We're stuck here in case some idiot tries to break in, but I'll be damned if I keep my hands to myself just because there's company."

"Whatever, man." Hemi pulled the blanket over his head and promptly passed out. His fading thoughts about sun-kissed skin, blonde hair and pale pink lips crashed into his dreams.

* * * *

He woke with a start, reaching out again, except this time he fell off the damn couch. His landing on the floor barely registered thanks to his cybernetic side making impact, though the surface beneath cracked a bit from his weight.

Shit, can't go a day without busting myself or something else.

Hemi glanced at the window against the wall and there was no light, just darkness. He pushed up on his knees, then used the couch to get to a standing position before he grabbed his cane. The world seemed a bit off kilter, as if he'd slept for too long.

There were voices coming from the bay, the sound of tools clanging, maybe a water torch and a welder, swear words accompanied with laughter. Naturally, Hemi moved out of Snapper's office and toward the noise.

"He's not going to be ready to drive. You know that right?" This came from Snapper. The bass of his voice had the hair on Hemi's neck standing on end.

Gina's tsk and sigh came before her words. "We can't be sure. Besides, you're discounting Jack and Hemi's determination. He's come so far."

"He slept all day. One day of pushing himself working on an engine and he's useless for almost twenty-four hours. Stamina and him holding up is an issue. We can't smooth that over."

"Enough!" Drag's voice was the closest and coming closer. "No more debates about it."

The Full Throttle leader walked right past Hemi, standing in the doorway of Snapper's office, and proceeded to the main entrance. "No use speculating or tearing someone down. We all do what we can."

The door creaked open and he heard Drag stop short. "I've done all I can. Now we wait for someone to test it. If he's not back in a couple days, then I'll climb in the damn thing myself."

The door was halfway shut when he heard Drag say, "Jack."

Snapper was jogging toward the door, Gina on his heels. Hemi followed.

Whatever emotions got churned up by their comments were swept away with relief knowing Jack and Shannon had returned. The mission might have been a success or not, but he didn't care. To know they were both safe, to have Shannon come back and hopefully help him finish his rehab.

Jack would understand what was happening with him right now. *He'll get it.*

Hemi got outside to find Jack on a uni-rider. A Skeiron-based one, judging from the slither carved into the engine cover. Jack was covered with dirt, looked like hell. His clothes were equally dirty, and there were specks of blood on him.

Amid all the others talking, Hemi found his relief dying away. "You bastard, we were worried… Where's Shannon?"

* * * *

Two hours later and Hemi found himself standing at the corner of Jack's place waiting. He hadn't gone home, was damn aware he probably smelled like ass and looked it. But ever since he'd left Jack and the crew in the Watering Hole, he'd been in the training facility, lifting, pounding the bag and feeling guilty for not pushing himself to go with them.

He wanted to believe Jack had done the right thing, just as he'd said before he'd left the group. But instead, Hemi found himself contemplating the worst of his friend. Why did he care so much?

Because she's the only one, besides Sophia, that treated you like you weren't a freak.

That didn't count Snapper and Drag because those two and even Gina still viewed him as someone weak, to be coddled. He didn't need that.

He also couldn't face Sophia yet. Not until he knew where Shannon was.

Jack stepped up to his front door, a hushed, "Fuck," coming out as he gripped the doorknob handle.

Hemi rolled his shoulders and walked up behind him. They were going to talk or fight—he wasn't sure which.

"Suggest you open the door so we can have this conversation inside versus out." Hemi's voice came out with a low growl. Though his anger was present, it might have been misguided.

Jack opened the door. "You've got questions, I'll answer them."

He left it ajar so Hemi could follow him inside. Jack lit a lamp and turned the heat element on low. Hemi found the room a lot homier than his, with a few knickknacks, pictures and aesthetic objects that Hemi had never bothered with.

He shut the door behind him and turned the lock. "Tell me what you did and why she didn't come back."

* * * *

Sophia should have felt bad for spying and listening at doors, but when Hemi failed to come home the night prior and she was unable to gain access to the Full Throttle mechanics bay, dismissed by Snapper that Hemi was fine and just working, she'd become desperate.

Then Hemi had intensified her fears talking about a woman named Shannon. Not once, not twice, but thrice. Her name had spilled from his lips outside the bay as she waited for a mere glimpse of him, inside the Watering Hole where they'd all gathered around to celebrate the return of another cyborg, Jack.

Then he had said her name again, just now inside Jack's domicile. Sophia truly had no idea who Hemi was anymore and maybe she'd misjudged the situation all along.

Why did he make that offer?

The little crack in her resolve emerged anew, made bigger by Hemi's desertion. Teija's mention of her selfishness replayed. Had she forced this on Hemi? Made him act against his own desires? If he loved Shannon...

"I fell for her." The muffled voice from inside wasn't Hemi's. She recognized the different pitch, just an octave or so higher.

"Yeah, figured you would." Hemi's response made Sophia's heart pound. *Does that mean?*

"I know you care about her, and I get I moved in..."

Sophia turned and left as quietly as she came, off the steps and onto the worn dirt road that served as the one of the paths through town. She didn't want to hear any more. Because she wanted to be selfish for one more day, to cling to the fantasies she'd let grow in her heart.

Ones that had been nourished when she'd seen Hemi again at the regional race months prior.

He'd been a driving warrior, honored, revered, and once he won the race, she truly believed he would make his claim for her. He'd gone all the way, then the accident...the racer had erupted into flames and flipped. Sophia had almost lost hold of her dreams then.

She'd given up until the rumors among the trading caravans in Aurestral had started sharing news of a driver who'd been turned into a half cyborg and saved from near-death. Though, in the wake of her father's decree for her marriage, she'd really believed the opportunity to see Hemi again would never present itself. *How lucky...only he's in love with someone else.*

She reached Hemi's front door and stood there for a moment, shocked that in her blind musing she'd still found her way back to his home. To the place he'd earned.

He's come so far from hiding in corners and scavenging for scraps.

Their past was tightly intertwined, and she'd taken that connection for granted, believing the ties that bound them would surpass anything. She had walked into his town, barged her way inside his life, without even considering his emotions were engaged elsewhere.

You're as bad as your father, Sophia.

And maybe twice as ruthless. That was what she might have thought, but it didn't stop her from slipping into one of Hemi's sleeveless shirts and a pair of loose knit pants.

Selfish for one more night.

She traced the lines of the Full Throttle tattoo. The one inked over her gang's three stars. A foolish decision, but one she wouldn't regret even if Teija turned her over and her fiancé desired retribution.

I won't let Hemi pay for my mistakes. Not now, not ever.

The slamming of the front door had Sophia bolting out of the bed. She scrambled to a sitting position and prepared for the worst. Her heart raced as she worried that Teija had already been dispatched to bring her home before she'd even had a chance to accomplish more than discovering how silly she'd been in believing Hemi had secret feelings for her.

But instead of someone barging into the bedroom, the heavy footsteps stomped and dragged toward the kitchen.

Hemi.

She got out of bed and headed toward the noise. Hemi leaned against a counter drinking a glass of recycle, then put something small in his mouth with his other hand.

"Are you all right?"

"No, my sleep schedule is off, and I just sent a friend charging out after he's barely had any time to recover from nearly dying. But I need to get back to the mechanics bay and..." Hemi trailed off as his gaze finally met hers then perused her body. "You're wearing my clothes."

"It was easier and I..." She could say how she wanted to be close to him, wanted to hold on to a part of him even as she knew she'd have to give him up. "I'm sorry."

"I wasn't saying it was a bad thing, just surprised me." Hemi went silent and they both stood there.

Ridiculous how she felt awkward in front of him when before she'd been so sure. "I'm sorry for a lot more than this." She plucked at the sleeveless shirt. "I saw you earlier...with Jack and talking about Shannon."

He stood up a little straighter, setting his glass to the side. "What do you mean?"

Joseph's balls... She'd have to tell him the entire thing, wouldn't she? "I was in the Watering Hole when you all came in. I needed food and you didn't seem to plan on coming home ever, so I went there for a meal. Then you were distracted and afterwards I noticed you went to Jack's... I came here thinking you and I—"

"Let's just nip this right here. You didn't do the wrong thing coming here and Shannon is...someone I care about but it's not..." His hesitation scared her, made her more nervous, enough so that she was digging her fingernails into her palms.

"Just speak plainly. You don't have to cushion your words. I can handle whatever you have to say." She wasn't sure why she'd confessed such a thing to him. Though it appeared he already worried about her feelings when this whole marriage between them was supposed to be fake anyway. He didn't want her hurt, meaning she was already exposed.

"Fine. I liked her, but it's never going to be anything between us because Jack loves her and she... Well, she better love him."

"You won't fight for her?" The question was damn loaded because she recalled the day Hemi disappeared from Aurestral. *The day he left me.*

"I can't fight for a person who wants someone else."

"You don't know that." Did she sound a little higher pitched? Needy? Her heart raced because there were words that she couldn't say without making this even more awkward. After the morning a couple days ago, she didn't want Hemi to disappear on her again.

"Oh, I know enough. There is plenty Jack didn't say, but it's not important."

"You dismiss yourself too easily." She moved as she spoke, coming closer to him out of frustration. "Why do you put aside what you want for others without a second thought? It's okay to be a little selfish, Hemi."

Isn't that exactly what Teija accused me of? And I want to bring him to my level.

"I think I've been plenty selfish, and making the offer I did proves it. You should have left the morning after. Taken whatever out Teija offered, and instead you stayed. Whether that's for me or not, I don't know. But crazily enough, I could hope."

She froze at those words because they were as close to a confession as she'd gotten from him that her feelings weren't all one-sided.

Unfortunately, a knock at the front door, a sound she was beginning to hate down to the marrow in her bones, halted any conversation. She was so close to touching him and she reached for his cybernetic arm now, to band her hands to him and keep him still. He pulled away before she could fully latch on and moved toward the door.

A part of her didn't believe those words he'd said. The fact he'd let someone at the front door interrupt them made her second-guess if she'd heard him right.

He opened the door and she couldn't see who stood on the other side. Sophia wanted to tune out whatever was being said, provide a sliver of privacy, but she didn't miss the gruff tone or the name *Jack* and *need*.

"I'll be there within the solar hour." Hemi shut the door then and turned to face her. The sigh he let loose said enough.

"Work's never done, right?" She mustered a smile, even if she couldn't feel any joy for not being able to talk with Hemi more.

"No, it never is. They need me, and…just promise you'll get with Gaia. Let her give you the tour, and work on figuring stuff out. I may be gone for a couple days."

She nodded her agreement and decided to stay in the main room as Hemi moved into his bedroom and disappeared. She was on her own again, left to figure out where her future lay.

Chapter Eight

A whole day had passed, and Sophia had hidden inside Hemi's house for most of it. She'd even skipped dinner and focused on sleeping. Lots of rest, amid nightmares and futile dreams. She awoke sobbing, while other times trying to tear the very covers from his bed. Regardless, every time she'd opened her eyes, she'd been alone.

Alone. A word that echoed in her mind and crawled like a slither, infecting her with restlessness. When had she ever truly been left to her own devices, with no demands upon her time, no expectations weighing her down? She didn't know how to act in the face of inaction.

As the sun rose on the second day of no Hemi, she showered and dressed. Pulling her hair back, she covered it out of respect for Teija and his concern over her safety, though it wasn't much of a disguise. She experienced a little bit of guilt as well because Teija might be blamed for her rebellious determination to avoid the match.

Can't change things now. She sighed and took a deep breath, preparing herself to face the day. Then she slipped on her boots, clacking the heels together like she used to do whenever she'd leave her room growing up. She marched down the street, ready to show up at the Watering Hole and get Gaia to show her around Frog Lick.

Except, what if I see Hemi inside?

"Hey, hey…Sophia, is it?" A female voice had Sophia pivoting on her heel to come face to face with a mythical creature. At least the woman looked like something straight out of a tale told by the story weaver in Aurestral. She stood barely to Sophia's shoulder, her brown skin covered with freckles and hair so curly the strands looked like coiled racer shocks. Her hair was dark, like the Marsanium ore they pulled from the ground.

"Yeah, that's my name."

"Good. It's so nice to get to introduce myself. I'm Petal."

The name was lost on her, and Sophia stood still for a moment, blinking repeatedly trying to recall who this woman was.

"Rune's wife?"

Rune was the brother of Drag, Full Throttle's leader and the man who'd witnessed her marriage ceremony to Hemi. He'd mentioned several times how the union reminded him very much of his and Petal's.

"Right, so sorry. The last few days have been a whirl."

Petal grinned. "I imagine. Hemi does have that way about him, though I know things right now are a little busy. What with the rescue and all."

Rescue? Sophia was tempted to inquire but decided against being nosy. If there were problems, her curiosity would only raise concerns instead of alleviating them. She knew how paranoid gang-towns got with outsiders. Even though Hemi had made her a member through marriage, she still needed to prove herself.

"Join me for breakfast then?" Better to start to get to know people, because if Hemi kept up with his avoidance act, she'd be on her own a lot more.

That's what you said you wanted. Of course, she'd lied. She wanted a future like what Petal appeared to have with Rune. A meaningful existence where she could help those around her. Where she could help those in Aurestral and get rid of the differences that made Hemi believe he couldn't be with her either.

"Sure, Gaia has a new recipe she's been trying with the oats we produced in the airponics bay." Petal led the way into the Watering Hole and Sophia followed. "How are you settling in?"

"I'm..." —*lonely, worried my father's going to send Teija to bring me home, frustrated*— "still trying to get used to how things work here."

"Well, if you have time, we can definitely show you around."

"Gaia offered something similar."

Petal grinned. "Of course, she did." The shorter woman looped her arm through Sophia's, and with a gentle tug, took them straight to a couple of bar stools.

The noise level was similar to the previous times she'd entered during work hours. Only a few patrons here and there, scarfing down food and engaging in quiet conversation. Everything about this place spoke to the area being beyond a bar and less about getting drunk — more about quality meals and collaboration.

"Got those oats ready?"

"Soaked and paired up with some of those berries you've been growing," Gaia replied as she slid a couple small bowls toward them with spoons already placed. "I think I can break away for that tour I promised after you eat."

Sophia blinked to make sure she was seeing the woman in front of her. "But...did Hemi?"

Gaia grinned. "Did he what? I know I promised you a look at the town a couple days ago and haven't quite lived up to my promise. Blame me for thinking you needed a little more time to settle in, but now...with your guard gone, seems like this might be for real."

So, others had doubted her commitment to Hemi and to Full Throttle. Teija leaving had signaled to Full Throttle and Frog Lick she was going to stay.

Wish I would have known that sooner.

She tucked some strands of hair behind her ear and picked up the spoon. "Yeah, it is. I want to learn more about this place I plan to call home."

Deep down, she meant those words and her chest got tight as she scooped up a spoonful of brown mush and a small black ball. She'd never enjoyed oats before, at least not for breakfast, and berries weren't high on their list either. At least not black ones. The ones her family propagated were deep red, harvested from bushes that grew in a private airponics bay and were dried out for rehydration. Rarely had she ever eaten fresh fruit.

It's extravagant.

Those were the only words to describe the rich, tart flavor that coated her mouth as she bit into the berry, mixing both bitter and sweet with the oats. There was a tiny bit of a gritty mouth-feel, but overall the experience was new and refreshing.

She scooped up one bite after another, fast and quick, ensuring each one came with a berry. "This is delicious."

"I agree with Sophia, though the oats may need more washing next time. More bitter than the last round," Petal added in between her own bites.

Gaia just shook her head. "Can't please everyone. Meet me out front when you're done."

It didn't take Sophia that long—only three more bites—and she found herself tempted to lick the bowl. Her mother would have exclaimed in horror and her father would have given his frequently used disapproving cluck, so she decided to do what her heart desired. She shoved her face in the bowl and giggled in between licks as some of the leftover bits got on her nose and cheek.

When she finally pulled the bowl back after a successful cleaning, Petal was holding a square of fabric out to her and grinning. "What was all that about?"

"Tasted so good, I wanted to clean up what was left but the spoon wasn't enough. I've never been allowed to do that before."

"Lick your dishes?"

"Yeah."

Petal started to laugh and in turn Sophia joined her. It was good to think of the silliness of this entire interaction dispelling the sad truth that Sophia had been raised to believe herself above such small forms of pleasure. Putting a tongue to dishes or sitting in a common bar room. Eating a meal prepared by someone unknown and not a vetted approved cook. There were so many parts of her experience thus far that she would never have been able to have at home.

She tucked an arm around her belly. Her stomach ached from how hard she laughed. But as the boisterous noise died down, she noticed a few people looking at them and Sophia became very conscious of drawing bad attention in her direction.

"It is silly, isn't it?"

"No, you're from Aurestral, right? In the Aurora region?"

Sophia nodded, though she hoped confessing such a thing wouldn't endanger her in the future.

"I've heard things are quite different there. Gang-towns with buildings stacked on one another, and the gang leaders get treated more like royalty."

Guilt tightened in her belly now, replacing her happiness with a sour discontent. She'd lived a fancy life in comparison to others. One she could now view was privileged and sheltered. "I'm sorry."

"Don't apologize. You're here now."

Sophia glanced at the woman, daring to hold her amber gaze. "Doesn't change my past."

"It changes your future. Pasts only matter if you dwell in them. I'm sure Hemi told you Full Throttle has some different philosophies around a woman's place in the world."

"Hard not to see it firsthand what with Gaia being the proprietor of the bar here. I'm sure that wasn't the case previously."

"You're right, it wasn't." Petal stacked her bowl with Sophia's then got off the stool. "Drag changed all that, and if you want, you can be part of that change. Learn a skill, a trade, and build yourself up to be more than a woman who's prevented from licking dishes and fed special meals."

The call was strong, like it possessed its own scent of earth and iron, rich with possibilities beyond a simple offer. This desire to be more than pampered and sheltered had sunk into her veins and grown a life of its own. She stood on a precipice, the same way she'd stood on that stage a few days prior and pledged her future to a man she'd loved since she was ten years old.

There's no turning back.

"I'm ready. Let's see this place."

* * * *

"Of course, you know where the mechanics bay is. The mines aren't far off, we have a shaft that goes into the area and it's sealed off, all safe. The shipping bay has been shut down and closed since...the incident. Then there's hydroponics and airponics. Which would you like to see first?"

Sophia had walked a couple of hours. They'd also viewed the school, the ore-processing building and the construction house, which was used to actively source materials and re-work parts for expansion and repairs of the buildings.

"Airponics because I enjoy good food and those berries this morning were delicious. I want to know more."

Minutes later, they walked past a barrier of sheeting and into an area of rows and rows of wooden boxes with various plants growing from them. Thick trunks with branches, tall grasses, stalks with various odd-shaped objects growing from them in a variety of colors. It was a bit overwhelming to see so many options when she'd barely interacted with food outside of eating what was prepared for her.

"What is all this?"

"This is my genius husband's mad idea to become a farmer come to fruition," Petal said as she twirled around in front of Sophia, arms spread wide motioning to the garden surrounding them.

"What's a farmer?"

Gaia chuckled. "It's an old Earth term. Hundreds of years ago, before the launch, men and women cultivated the land to grow their food. It wasn't synthesized or blended from proteins and modified vitamins. They grew it fresh, but in vast quantities. We're not that big yet, but thanks to Rune's ideas, we may get there."

"Where did you get all the plants?"

"From seeds collected on the planet Eden. Drag made an agreement with them, an exchange for some ore, and in return they provided the start to the airponics area."

They walked row to row, with Gaia and Petal providing more details. How hard work, dedication and a mixture of iron-rich soil and a nitrogen-infused spray had made the plants grow with irrigation techniques replicated from old Earth manuals Rune had bartered for from a trader. Sophia was standing in a marvel, one she could easily see sharing with the rest of the gang-towns. This would eliminate hunger, starvation. No more slums. No more adults trading their bodies for basic needs.

"And if the weather is poor or we're in the cold season, it's easy to elevate the sheeting you see lining the area. We can also protect everything at night from unpredictable weather. The sheeting is reinforced with a polymer compound we were able to get from the moonies."

Both Gaia and Petal stepped outside of the sheeting barrier and Sophia followed. She was trying to pay attention, but the sound of a hauler headed in their direction distracted her. They were speeding into town, not slowing, with at least three men.

"Ladies, I think there is a problem."

Petal turned toward Sophia, and had already taken a step forward when Gaia charged into them both, pushing them away from the road. "That's not a Full Throttle. It's Skeiron."

"From Auster?" Petal was suddenly on the move, running toward a nearby building. "We need to alert the town."

The hauler started to slow. Sophia could hear the purring of the engine weaken, then the unmistakable click and cock of guns.

"You three don't move or we shoot."

Chapter Nine

Metal rattled as someone pounded on the walls of Hemi's training building.

What the hell?

He pushed himself to a standing position, forgetting his cane and moving toward the front door. When he reached it, the metal frame wrenched open and there stood Gaia panting. Her hair was mussed, braids disturbed and sweat dripped down her face.

"Hemi, they took her," she said between heavy breaths.

"Took who? Who are they?" Dread clenched against his chest, the same way it had the instant before his entire body caught on fire in the accident. He'd known seconds beforehand he was going to have an accident and there was nothing he could do. Now, he stood here again wondering—"Is it Shannon? Does Macintosh have her?"

Gaia's frown was immediate and intense. "Shannon...why the hell are you worried about her? Sophia! They took Sophia."

She reached for him and clasped his shoulders, attempting to shake him with no luck. "They were Skeiron and they mean to ransom her. Knew exactly who to look for, too...the Aurestral princess."

Fuck!

Hemi took a step back and near-fell. He stumbled a couple steps then regained his footing. The damn cybernetic leg was not as responsive as he needed it to be. "What direction did they head out of town?"

"East, of course. For the Auster border, I imagine."

Hemi made it to his cane, snatched up the rod and headed for the door. "Have the others been alerted?"

"We were at the airponics bay. I made it here first."

Of course, she had. Hemi's training place was closer to airponics than the mechanics bay. "I'll tell them, just head to the Watering Hole. We'll meet you there."

But Snapper and Gina had given everyone the afternoon off. With Jack gone again, no doubt that influenced it. Hemi couldn't find either of them, except Drag.

"You sent him running out after Shannon, couldn't keep your mouth shut for two minutes," Drag said as soon as he saw Hemi.

This wasn't their first conversation about this mess. No, Drag had already read him the riot act that morning. Especially when it was confirmed the blood amount Jack had left them with wasn't enough to solve their cybernetic issues.

"We have a bigger problem right now. Skeiron just entered Frog Lick and kidnapped Sophia."

Drag's entire frame locked, his grip on the doorframe of Snapper's office splintering the wood. "Your wife got kidnapped in our territory?"

"Yes, and we have to get her back."

Drag pushed him aside and headed for the nearest hauler. "Climb in and direct me on the way. This shit won't stand. I'm sick and tired of having to prove ourselves to the damn gangs within Wespero, but now an Auster gang tries to pull this shit."

A click of a button and the bay doors were spreading wide to make room for their departure. Hemi gave up trying to haul his disproportioned body over the door like he would have done time and time again before the accident, opting to open the door and climb inside.

"Still not quite moving as agile as you'd like. Those second-gen nanites would be a big help probably."

"You're never going to let me live that down, are you?" Hemi's question was almost drowned out by the roar of the hauler's engine as Drag fired it up.

"Sorry, didn't quite catch that."

The exchange wasn't lessening Hemi's anxiety as he gripped the cane top until his knuckles hurt. Instead of arguing more about something he couldn't change, Hemi chose to focus on the necessary info to rescue Sophia. Sophia who'd he'd been ignoring like an idiot.

If they hurt her…

"She was with Gaia and Petal at the airponics bay. Gaia said they were probably headed toward Auster territory."

Drag nodded and gunned it right as the creak of the metal bay doors halted. "Then we take the quickest route to follow."

Wind whipped at his skin as Drag pushed the hauler to speeds most wouldn't dare, except for maybe himself and Jack. They were drivers through and through. It made Hemi a little jealous at how easy Drag could do what Hemi believed would be impossible for him now. Hemi couldn't lie and say he didn't miss being in a vehicle charging down a stretch of clear space, road or otherwise.

They were passing the outlying buildings and making a sharp right near the ship-building bay in under a minute.

"Now, while we catch up, tell me the rest of the details." Drag's gaze never left the road, hands locked on that steering wheel and deftly maneuvering them around rocks, plants, and other small obstacles as they cleared out of Frog Lick and into open territory.

"According to Gaia, there were three men on a hauler. Not sure on size, but Sophia went willingly to ensure Gaia and Petal weren't hurt, and they were armed."

Drag readjusted his hold on the wheel. "Helpful information, though not what I'm talking about. Tell me why Sophia is so important they took her?"

They had yet to have this conversation and Hemi was a bit of a sludge-sack to think it would never happen. He'd hoped to wait until after Jack had returned before having to explain Sophia's past to Drag and the potential problems her presence could bring to Full Throttle.

He tapped the tip of the cane against the floorboard once, then twice. "We grew up together."

"Yeah, and I was born with two human arms. Quit chasing the bobtail scratcher and spit it out. I see their dust trail in the distance. Won't take long to be upon them and your explanation is the only thing that might determine if I finish this pursuit."

The firm, no-nonsense tone was as rough as Drag had ever gotten with Hemi. In ways it made it easier to take because Hemi had plenty of things he wanted to voice to Drag, but never the right moment or right time. Not when Drag acted so damn remorseful about putting Hemi in the racer.

It should have been me.

Those words were repeated to Hemi periodically during his recovery. Except, in this moment he refused to feel guilty for his choices.

"She's the daughter of the gang leader for Aurestral."

The hauler's engine hiccupped for a split second, the only implication that Hemi's words had an effect on Drag.

How much should I say? "She came here at first just wanting to see if I was alive, and then I wanted to help my friend. We were close growing up. She got me a mentorship in their mechanics bay because I saved her life. When she told me how her parents were trying to force her to marry someone she didn't know —"

"A Skeiron?"

Hemi frowned. "I was drunk when she told me, but I don't think so. No, it was another gang. She asked for my help, and she already saved me..."

Hell, the excuses were weak, emotional, but wasn't that how Full Throttle operated? On what was best for the gang, but also on feelings.

"If you're going to turn back, drop me off and I'll follow on foot. I owe her that much not to let her get kidnapped by those pointy-toothed, slither-worshiping bastards. But if you were willing to send Jack on a potential fool's errand to save five of us, then I would hope you can understand what my debt to Sophia means."

They were silent for a bit and now Hemi could see what Drag had. The dust trail more prominent as they got closer, the outline of the hauler and of at least three people in the vehicle.

She probably doesn't have sun goggles or anything to protect her skin.

Silly of him to be worried about minor things when there were more urgent concerns. "Well?"

Drag sighed, and the hauler accelerated a bit more. "Wish I would've known this right after your marriage ceremony. I feel a little blind-sided, but we'll get her from Skeiron. Though once her parents find out, her intended as well, and every gang in between...we could have bigger problems on our hands. Ones that outweigh any debt you have when I have an entire gang to think about."

"I know that."

"Yeah, you say you do and yet you didn't think you could trust me with this. Didn't think to come and ask for my help, but instead thought your only solution was marrying her?"

Hemi opened his mouth then shut it again. Drag wasn't wrong in his statement. There were other options, but Hemi had chosen the most selfish one of them all because it seemed right at the time, and he refused to analyze the others.

The most glaring one was his desire to get back at Sophia's father. That decree, *"You'll never marry my daughter,"* still played havoc on him years later. If Hemi hated anything, it was being told what to do by someone who didn't respect him.

"I thought it was the best move at the time, so I went with it."

"Well, maybe next go-around remember you're not alone in everything. I thought we chatted about this before. You have people who want to help you."

And I wouldn't need help if you'd just let me die.

Hemi couldn't say those words out loud because if he'd died, then Sophia would be married to a person she didn't know, Jack would have left Shannon behind…the trickle-down effect was too great to even contemplate.

"I'll try to remember next time."

Drag slapped the steering wheel. "I hope so. Now, get in the storage box there in the underside of the dash. Should be a flare gun. You think once I get up on this vehicle, you can land a shot in their rear driver side tire well?"

"Won't that flip the hauler?"

"They have weapons and they aren't going to stop if we pull up alongside and ask them to."

Hemi opened the door to the box and grabbed the flare gun. "If it flips and they don't have safety straps…"

The possibilities were numerous and ranged from superficial to death. If Sophia died in the process of him trying to save her… She hadn't asked for him to come chasing after her, just like he'd never asked for someone to replace half his body with cybernetic components.

"Make your decision quick. I'll be in range within the next minute. If you don't take the shot, then we won't be able to get her and I'll be dropping you right here."

Do I risk our lives to stop Skeiron? As if she'd somehow sensed his worrisome thoughts, he could have sworn she glanced over her shoulder and stared at him, but it was near impossible to see with the amount of dust kicking up around them at the speeds they were traveling.

Hemi wanted to believe she nodded at him as he held the gun aloft, the distance between the two haulers closing as they reached a decent stretch of wide-open land with less wildlife.

Please let me be right.

He aimed and waited.

"Fire now!"

At Drag's command, Hemi took a deep breath, refocused and squeezed the trigger on the exhale. His cybernetic right arm worked, for once in its existence, with no recoil as the flare launched and hit the target. The impact did exactly what Hemi had believed would happen. The entire hauler flipped. One of the occupants went flying out, while the other two stayed inside the vehicle.

"Hold on!"

Hemi gripped the door, the metal underneath his cybernetic fingers crunching with his hold as Drag eased up on the accelerator then made a sharp turn to point them back in the direction toward Frog Lick.

"Do you think she was the one that went flying?"

Hemi wanted to believe Sophia was smart enough to buckle herself in when riding in a hauler. "No, I don't think so."

"Then to the hauler we go, but we're wasting precious time if it was her. Whoever launched is definitely hurt badly."

Hemi was well aware of the stakes. "She's in the vehicle. Let's be quick."

They started to slow down. Before Drag could even bring the hauler to a complete stop, Hemi was rolling out of the vehicle.

Time to see whether this stupid cybernetic-infused body can do a damn thing.

Chapter Ten

Sophia didn't want to move. Not when she was nice and warm, safe with Hemi. Hemi...she hadn't gotten to say goodbye, then those pointy-toothed jerks had put her in the hauler at gunpoint.

Warm, but not nice.

She started to cough then forced her eyes open.

"Sophia."

She batted away the hand reaching for her. Hard metal, cold to the touch.

"Don't fight me. Can you undo the safety strap?"

When Sophia blinked a couple times, the haze of dust around her cleared a bit along with the itchiness, though now her vision was blurry because of the excess water her tear ducts were generating. Still she could make out—

"Hemi?"

"Yes, princess. I'm here. Can you release the safety strap so I can help you get out of here?"

Sophia slid her arm down along her side trying to stifle her discomfort as a sharp pain radiated through the same limb. It took pressing her two fingers against the button to finally hear the tell-tale click.

Then the drop, a sudden jerk in movement as she plunged from her seat, hanging upside down, toward the rocky ground. She closed her eyes tight, praying the fall didn't hurt her more…except instead of hard ground, she landed in a pair of arms.

The breath she'd been holding came out on a sigh.

"Don't worry, I got you, but it's going to be a little bumpy the next couple minutes. Tuck your head close to my chest and hold on tight."

Hemi wasn't lying. Every shimmy of his body backward from underneath the Skeiron hauler set off aches and pains within her body. When they finally got out from the hauler, there was still no relief in sight as Hemi readjusted his hold and pushed to a standing position.

"Just a little bit longer. I'll get you to a safe spot."

She kept her eyes closed to stem the nausea rising in her stomach, the radiating pain in her chest, the sharp stinging bites and tingles in her arms and legs. It was like her body had been railed upon. She briefly believed this was how Hemi and other drivers felt when getting in accidents with their racers.

"Sorry I ever suggested…this. I never knew."

Hemi's hold on her tightened. "I don't think you arranged a kidnapping."

"No, racing. It was so dangerous, and I suggested it all those years ago."

She had been in a bad way all those years ago. When he'd found her on the verge of being bullied by a group of starving gang orphans, he'd saved her. Then she'd believed she could repay him by getting him an apprenticeship with the mechanics bay, changing his future in a way that might give him more success.

"My choices, Sophia. Mine." He groaned and her body shifted lower.

"I'm too heavy."

He stopped for a moment. His breathing was labored.

She dared to open her eyes. Her goggles had fallen off her head in the crash. The bright light of the sun cast Hemi's face in shadow since it was angled down toward her. She could barely make out his features but could clearly see the sweat on his brow and cheeks. "Just put me down. Go get the hauler."

He shook his head. "No, I'll get you there."

She hesitated about arguing with him some more. Him killing himself to save her wasn't an option she wanted to consider. Yet he'd experienced setbacks since seemingly coming back to life after his accident. Hadn't he appreciated how she looked at him like he was a regular man? *Why not treat him like one?*

"You can do it. Stand the hell up and let's get moving."

He gazed down at her then smiled. "Is that a demand, princess?"

"A command. If you're going to play savior again, I can't have you give up now."

The words seemed to do the trick. He hoisted her again and she gritted her teeth at the renewed agony any movement put on her body, but she refused to let him know how much it hurt. In what seemed like too damn long, they made it to the hauler and Hemi laid her down in the second row of seating.

"It's not very comfortable and I imagine the ride back won't be. Do you think you can manage?"

She winced as she tried to reposition herself. "What are my options? I don't suppose asking you to knock me out is possible?"

Hemi frowned. "I'd never hurt you."

You already have.

He'd been hurting her since the moment they'd gotten married, and he continued to put distance between them. She was not supposed to be here for him, but herself. The lie she'd told only caused more of an issue, but she'd stupidly hoped proximity would change Hemi's mind. Though their differences might be too surmountable to bypass. She sat on some invisible pedestal that she never wanted or asked for.

"Sophia?"

Her vision blurred because, even with those barriers, he'd still come for her as she'd hoped. Hell, he'd put himself in harm's way for her. The Skeiron jerks hadn't told her who had hired them, only that she was worth enough flash to take care of their gang. Then they'd slapped her for her daring to speak.

Maybe Hemi was right to stay away from her. She didn't deserve a future outside of what was already promised, and any deviation was going to keep putting him in danger.

"Princess?" He reached for her, smearing a stream of her tears across her cheek with his thumb. "Tell me what's making you cry, and I'll fix it."

"You can't fix this. I'm a curse. Just causing problems ever since I got here."

Hemi lifted her chin between his thumb and forefinger. "Look at me."

She dared to open her eyes, blinking against the illumination from the sun until he stepped in and blocked most of it with the bulk of his body.

"You didn't ask for anything but my help. I swore I'd give it, but I've been scared. I won't be any longer."

"What if I want more?"

He leaned in, closing the gap between them, even though they were faced in opposite directions. "What do you want?"

"For starters, a kiss."

A light chuckle emerged from him and for a minute she could forget whatever aches her body suffered from. "I thought I gave you one of those already?"

"I forgot."

"Hemi!"

He stood up straight and she put a hand over her eyes to protect them. "One second. I need to go see what he wants. We get you back to Frog Lick and checked out and as soon as you have the all clear... I promise you this, I'll make sure you never forget my kiss again."

Sophia sighed then winced at the traveling twinge in her ribcage and around to her back. Hemi was already gone, walking off to talk to whoever else was there. She should leave well enough alone, not strain herself or attempt further injury by sitting up yet...curiosity and her being raised to be a leader prevented her from remaining ignorant.

Grabbing a hold of the headrest, she hauled herself up with steady breathing and grinding her teeth together. A scoot and a shove later and she wedged herself against the left passenger door of the hauler, one hand gripping the bar on the door and the other the headrest.

She opened her eyes in short bursts to get her bearings, but not risk sun damage. *If I hadn't lost those fucking goggles.* She still had her head scarf and did her best to pull it lower around her cheeks to cover as much of her face as she could. Then she shielded her vision with her hands.

It took a few minutes, but she made out two people standing over what might have been a person or an animal. She recognized Hemi by his dark skin, and the other figure had to be Drag, with the silver shine of his arm. They'd traveled together to save her.

"We should question him!" She yelled and waited, still keeping up with her periodic opening of her eyes and closing them. No response came, at least not a verbal one.

Minutes passed, then the hauler jostled. She yelped as a heavy body fell against her shoulder, shoving her against the door.

"You're so interested in learning more about him, then you can share your seat." This came from Drag as he climbed into the driver's seat. "Buckle up."

"Don't be an ass, Drag." Hemi came to her side of the hauler and pushed the passed-out Skeiron off her. "Shouldn't have sat up. You could have a concussion."

"It was worth it," she said on a groan as Hemi locked her safety strap in place across her lap.

"Lucky you wore this the first time. You could've been killed when we fired that flare."

A thought she didn't care to give more time to. She was alive and that was what mattered now. "Whose great idea was it to flip the hauler to begin with?"

"Mine and you're welcome." Drag fired up the hauler then looked back at Hemi. "Are you done with your fawning? We need to move."

Hemi gave her cheek a gentle brush then moved to get in the front passenger seat. They raced back to Frog Lick. Every bump in the road seemed to rattle her bones, but eventually she found a lull and passed out.

* * * *

When Sophia woke, she was no longer in the hauler, but in Hemi's bed. She immediately recognized the scent on the sheets and the low-light lamps gave it away. The door to the bedroom was open a crack and she heard several voices in heated conversation.

"Did Drag get that bastard to talk?"

"Yeah, why did they want to take her?"

Sophia recognized Gaia's forceful, no-bullshit tone and Petal's gentle concern. Bracing her arms against the bed, Sophia tried to push herself up and winced at the lingering pain in her body as she got herself to a semi-upright position on the bed.

The temptation to call out to Hemi and the others was strong, but then Sophia recalled what her rescue had been like, the fear and frustration. How Hemi had risked himself for her and she shouldn't have been so damn happy about it. On top of the fact that he only came running to her side when she was in danger.

Reconciling her given reasoning for being in Frog Lick with her true desires was damn hard.

"I'll let you see her once she's had some rest. Gina already looked her over and she's doing fine. Thanks for your concern."

"If you don't tell me what I want to know, Hemi—"

"You'll go to Drag and I encourage you to. I'm busy with a patient and if you can't tell, I'm a little worse for wear myself."

Shit...is he hurt?

Her anxiety rose as fast as the temperature on the surface did during the day. Another thing she could blame herself for. *If only I'd never...no.*

Those were the type of mind games that only ever got her swirling. She'd had those thoughts before. If she were a boy, she wouldn't be forced into marriage. If she were smarter and more talented, her father would appoint her as his successor. If she had just told Hemi the truth...

"You're awake."

She jolted at the sound of Hemi's voice in the same room and glanced up to find him standing right across the threshold. She'd been so lost in her thoughts that she'd missed their guests leaving and even the opening of the bedroom door.

"Yeah, I woke up. Heard voices in the other room."

"You've been asleep since the ride back and it's been almost twenty-four hours. Gaia and Petal were worried." Hemi leaned against the door frame, taking the weight off his cybernetic side.

"Sounded like they were wondering what happened to my kidnapper." She patted the mattress. "You can come sit down if you need to. I can tell it's not very comfortable standing."

"Oh." He walked into the room, closer to her. But instead of the mattress, he chose a chair that was positioned next to the bed. "How can you tell?"

"You were leaning and you said as much to the women."

"Never mind me. How are you feeling?"

The answer was loaded because physically, she didn't really care but could tell nothing major was broken. Emotionally she was a damn mess, torn between guilt, happiness and the apprehension.

"Is it okay if I'm not able to say?"

Hemi leaned closer. "Are you hurting?"

"Yes and no, but let's talk about something else. Anything else."

"Then how about what you asked for before we had to stop talking?"

She swallowed hard, her throat going dry as the topsoil outside. Ridiculous that she'd been so deliriously out of it to ask him for the very thing she wanted him to give without her having to beg.

"I don't really remember much about what I said."

He chuckled and drew a thumb across his plump lips. "Then you don't recall asking me for a kiss?"

Fuck.

Chapter Eleven

Hemi could have used her fake memory lapse as an easy way out of this mess, but he needed a distraction. What better one than the woman he was officially bound to and who was willing to throw herself at him every chance she got?

He'd vowed to keep his hands off, to try to keep things from getting messy because eventually he'd be leaving Frog Lick and moving on. When that happened, she'd go back to Aurestral, to the life she'd been born to lead. He was a stepping stone, so why complicate that?

Because you've always wanted her and now is your chance.

Selfish wasn't quite how Hemi liked to describe himself, nor did he intentionally do whatever the hell he wanted because he'd learned over the years that doing what he desired had consequences.

Then again, he'd encouraged Jack to chase after Shannon. *He loves Shannon. Do I love Sophia?*

The idea made his gut churn and his chest tighten. When she'd been kidnapped, his only thought was to rescue her, to protect her. Her passed out in his bed for nearly twenty-four hours hadn't lessened this need to see her safe.

So, the kiss? Well, no sense backing away from it now. There would be no other chance. Not after Drag had his say. Hemi was already fucking things sideways by not letting Drag know she was awake now. This whole arrangement turned messy the moment she was kidnapped.

"Coon cat got your tongue?"

Sophia was all wide-eyed, mouth gaping open and shut like some sort of animal gasping for air. He almost started laughing but brought a hand to his mouth to stifle it.

"Maybe I underestimated my charm."

She shook her head then spoke, her voice softer than he'd ever heard it. "I just didn't want you to think I was like any other dust honey begging for attention. I mean, I know I'm forward sometimes, but..."

Her voice trailed off as he pushed out of the chair and came to sit beside her on the bed. Hemi tucked his index finger under her chin and gently nudged so he could be sure she was looking at him.

"You are wonderful when you're forward and asking for what you want. If you want to consider that dust honey material, then know this...those women have one thing going for them. They know what they want and they own it. Of course, what they want may be looked at by others in a negative light, but that kind of bravery doesn't come from nowhere."

"Isn't it degrading?"

"All depends on how you look at it." Hemi smiled. "But I see your flirting and asking as flattering. You're telling me that you'd rather have the lips of a half-human, cybernetic mess on you. That's humbling in a way."

She turned her head. "Yeah, but you could have anyone."

He couldn't let that stand, but he wouldn't force her to look at him. "Yet I was willing to bind myself to you. If that doesn't speak to what I want, I don't know what does."

"You said yourself...you did it to help me escape a future I didn't desire."

Hemi trailed those same fingers across her collarbone to her shirt-covered shoulder. His shirt. *Damn.* "Yeah, it's a good excuse. But you want me to talk, to truth-tell. If you want me to stop running, then I can say the future you want was only a reason to hide behind. One that got me more time with you. Though my guilt kept me away."

"What are you saying?" Her question came with a shiver. Her body rippled underneath his touch, and dust or bust, he wanted to see that happen again. Briefly, he pondered how she'd look coming apart beneath him. His cock grew hard.

Hell, I didn't even think such a thing still possible.

"I'm saying I want to kiss you if you'll let me. Maybe more if my body can handle it. Sophia, you're the most beautiful fucking woman I've ever seen."

She leaned toward him, her nose brushing against his. He gripped her upper arm to steady her as much as himself, letting out a sharp exhale.

"Say that again."

"Which part?"

"Tell me how you want me."

He grinned then let out a low growl. "Instead, I'll show you."

Finding her lips, melding his to hers wasn't a difficulty. A tender, hesitant touch at first but he didn't hesitate to trace the seam of her soft flesh, urging her open for him to delve into the unknown.

Sweet. She was sweet, unfurling to him like a flower seeking to reveal its beauty. He'd seen a few flowers in his lifetime, but none held as fond a memory as this moment would. When their tongues touched, it was like a tiny explosion of lust erupted and he was now a victim to the onslaught.

She let out a soft moan as she scooted closer, wrapping her arms around his body, closing whatever distance remained until she was flush against him, her breasts pressed to his chest. He almost forgot that part of him couldn't feel her there, so wrapped in the race between them. They were like racers on a track, in constant synchronized battle. Trying to find a way to coexist yet constantly at odds.

Her taste was uniquely her and something he couldn't identify, but damn if he didn't drown in some unseen scent that belonged solely to Sophia. *Sophia*. Her name was a prayer and a blessing because who cared if his body was imperfect. She didn't seem to.

Her hands started to roam freely across his body, arms, chest and lower. She gripped his hard cock with a firm hand and he tried to control himself. The sensations from her kissing and touching him were a little too much and his human side started to run hot.

Hemi broke away first. "Sophia, we need to slow for a minute."

"Why?" Her question came as she surged forward, seeking his lips again.

He held her back with his cybernetic hand, careful to not apply any pressure.

"Because I'm getting a little overheated. The cybernetic parts make me run a little hot anyway and I haven't…well…" How the hell did he stop being embarrassed about the fact he hadn't given it up since the accident?

"This is a first for you since the wreck?"

Point blank, then.

"Yes."

The wide-ass grin that took over her fast was nearly as mesmerizing as the woman herself. "Then you're technically a virgin."

"The fuck I am." He pulled her toward him. "I can damn well show you."

She laughed. "Still a man with an ego. I'm sure you've got moves. I just meant that the first time I have you will be the first time anyone has since your upgrade. Means you'll be all mine."

Those words hit him square in the solar plexus, like an invisible bomb exploding inside him, designed to launch chains to wrap around his heart. She'd declared ownership of him in a way that was thrilling because no one had wanted him as theirs. They'd wanted his sexual prowess, his cock, his tongue…but him as a whole, not so much. The him of now, with all this half metal, nanite-infected blood, and the real possibility he might never get further than what they just had.

"What we experienced could be it." He wasn't disillusioned to the truth. His body was still adjusting to this future state, and until Jack returned, there were worse things he might face.

"I've got time, we'll work things up slow." She palmed him again and he hissed at the friction she caused.

Devils, how he wanted more, wanted her naked, him naked... *Shit, she won't want to see my scarred body.* The metal bits of him, the puckered, burned flesh no longer his natural brown, but turned pink and white from surgery.

He was a monster, a damn patchwork mess under his clothes. "Maybe we take it real slow."

She gave him a nod before pressing a quick kiss to his lips. "Fine. I can go easy on you for the moment."

Hemi rebelled at this notion. Deep inside he wanted to throw caution to the wind because having her once would be everything. It would be a damn miracle if he lived through the experience. Instead, he forced himself still, determined to wait and be patient. Though he wasn't ready for her abrupt turn of focus.

"So, where is Drag keeping the man who kidnapped me?"

* * * *

Kissing Hemi had been better than any fantasy. After ten-plus years of daydreaming about the touch of lips that wasn't brief or on a cheek, they'd explored each other in a way that was better than anything she'd imagined.

Her disappointment at having to stop was buoyed by Hemi's confession of celibacy since the accident. Was she a little weird for being happy about that fact, a little selfish? Maybe, but since she'd already embraced and now confessed her reason for being here...okay, maybe not confessed, but she'd admitted to wanting him.

In her eyes, she'd come far from the day she'd walked into Frog Lick searching for him, but putting all the blame on her selected future. After Hemi had confirmed he preferred her forthright nature, it wouldn't take long for her to confess the rest. How she'd rebelled for him, wanted him to be the man she was married to. She could do this, but first she needed to figure out why and who had been behind her kidnapping.

"I don't think you need to worry about that. Drag is taking care of it."

"Yes, but if that happened because of my previous fiancé or my parents..." Hemi's gaze stopped her from finishing that sentence.

"Why would your parents be involved in this?"

"Teija left. You saw him leave. He was going to go home, I'm pretty sure, and once my parents find out, they will send someone."

Hemi clenched his hands, the grind of his metal-on-metal fingers a little concerning. "They wouldn't try to kidnap you... Sophia, I need to tell you the truth. My accident wasn't a simple mishap. Someone rigged the racer to explode with me in it. Full Throttle hasn't exactly announced who they suspect, but it's only a matter of time before we're at war."

"You're saying this might have been a ploy by another gang-town. One from Auster?" She found that a little difficult to process since that would imply gang-towns outside of Aurestral were communicating with each other. Her father had believed himself to be unique.

"I don't know. Seems a little far-fetched that the alternative is your parents would have you kidnapped instead of just coming for you."

She pushed the sheet that covered her back and rotated until her feet were flat on the floor. "Then I need to find out."

"No." Hemi reached for her, but she easily evaded him and hopped to a standing position. "Wait, you need rest."

"I slept for a day." And her body was still sore, but she'd forget about her physical woes for a minute. Especially if it meant determining how much time she had left, because they would come. No doubt forever was not possible here.

She glanced around the room. "Where are my boots?"

"Out by the door. You don't have to be so quick to try to get answers. We can wait a little."

She shook her head and reached for a pair of her pants from the bag she still had on the floor.

Keeping her focus on her pants, she opted for more truth telling. If Hemi truly enjoyed the side of her that was brutally honest about her wants, her desires, then she'd find out pretty fast if that was true.

"Listen, you're right. I could climb back in that bed and curl up beside you, but if I do, I'll want more of exactly what you said we had to go slow with. So let me have this chance to allow you to cool down and for me to find some answers."

As she finished speaking, she secured the snap on her pants and turned to find Hemi's darkened gaze watching her.

Those words had affected him. Her excitement grew anew. She was a racer, engine primed and ready to fly down a straightaway at the slightest press on the accelerator. *Except he said go slow.*

Hemi licked his lips and she didn't miss the hard swallow. "You're not going by yourself."

A glance out of the window showed the sun was still up. "It's afternoon, but we've got a few hours before the light fades. How about you follow, but go get your physical training in?"

He stood from the bed and approached her like a feral bob-scratcher hunting prey. She didn't mind being a target, but if they kissed again... "Hemi, the sooner you get that body in fit form, then—"

"Talking about how much you wanna fuck me isn't helping."

She pretended to seal her lips by dragging two fingers across them. "Then I'm done chatting. Is Drag at the mechanics bay or somewhere else?"

"Shipping bay on the edge of town." Hemi furrowed his brows as he looked her over.

"There's already extra security set, I'm sure?"

"Of course, but I'll still escort you over there."

She leaned in and gave him a kiss on the cheek. "Then lead the way."

Chapter Twelve

The walk to the shipping bay was quiet. Sophia reveled in being able to walk side-by-side with Hemi and not have him shying away from her.

When they reached the entrance, she stopped right inside the bay doors and turned to face him. "When do you want to meet?"

"I'll find you at Gaia's, how about that?" His voice was quiet as he gathered her hands in his sole human one. The other gripped the hand of his cane.

"You can walk without that. I know you can, saw you do it when you came to get me then carried me to the hauler."

Hemi chuckled. "Yeah, and I almost dropped you. Do you recall that? Don't lift me up like some deity when I have no way of living up to the ideal you're creating in your head. I'm flawed, greedy and weak."

She flexed her hands against his hold, loving how his body reacted to grip her tighter. "Then we're the same. Because I embody those traits, too. Regardless, I'll believe in you always."

Her words had the effect she wanted, Hemi standing a little taller, leaning a bit less. Regardless of how weak he viewed himself, he'd only succeed by believing he could. If there was one thing she could hope to offer him in her time here, besides her body, it was to re-instill faith in himself. *One positive word at a time.*

When he didn't say anything right away, Sophia moved to disengage from his hold. "Guess I'm off."

"Wait." Hemi readjusted his grip and pulled her close to him. "Don't try to tell Drag what to do. I know you'll mean well, but he's in charge here. Let him work the way he needs to and ask your questions, but that's it."

She had hoped for a kiss, not a warning. "Fine, I'll do my best."

"All anyone can ask for." He kissed her, but on the forehead, a light peck of the lips that was more chaste than what she longed for.

Later.

When they were alone again at his place, she'd angle for a little more, similar to their make-out session earlier. She stifled a giggle at the desperation of her thoughts and need for him as she walked off. Always the wanton for Hemi, she truly thought it funny how she'd throw herself at him any which way and instead of despising herself, she'd let his previous words lift her spirits up.

"I like you the way you are." He'd said as much.

The ship bay was a cavernous monstrosity with multiple ships in various stages of development. The metal structure with its Marsanium-hued interstellar beasts reminded her of a tomb. Instead of dead bodies, it housed the carcasses of dead people's dreams, the hunger pangs from their bellies.

If a gang-town can't build, they can't survive. Her father truly believed that, and Aurestral was one of the richest regions, supplying the most ships to the Uppers. Though Wespero had never been far behind. Her father had spoken quietly a few years ago about his fears of the Smith gang. How Frog Lick might surpass Aurestral in terms of quality.

Here lay the remnants of those concerns. Because Aurestral had celebrated the night Bebe Smith had been arrested and again the day the decree came down that Frog Lick and the gang residing within would have their ship-building rights revoked for ten years due to the Smiths' crimes against humans and the Allied Planetary Union. The Mars Shipping Commission had to issue a severe punishment to prove to the APU that Mars was worthy of being admitted, to having a voice in parliament for the first time since the colonization of the galaxy.

Sophia's steps slowed as she marveled at the shining frames, the rivets, the sleek outer walls, like the shells of eggs that encased and protected.

"They're beautiful, wouldn't you agree?"

Drag's voice echoed around her as he approached, but no sound came from his footsteps. The man was an anomaly. Gorgeous, gruff and with specks of blood across his dingy green shirt. She tried to focus on his face and not give away the concern she possessed for the captive.

"I would. Though a shame you're unable to continue building."

He stopped in front of her, then she noticed the blood on the knuckles of his human hand, too.

"Appreciate those words, though I'm sure your father would disagree. The Smith gang was once his biggest competition. We're two years down on the ten-year sentence. Once we win the championship, we'll be able to keep things going for the remaining eight. All our mining efforts and storage will set us up nicely and our engineers are already mapping designs. I can say the pause will put us in a good place to launch strong."

Sophia found Drag's words inspiring. No wonder he'd endeared himself to this entire town. His optimism was infectious. He'd been selected as their leader because he had a vision and was carving it out the same way a ship engineer drafted the plans for a vessel.

"Sounds like you know what you want."

"I do, and I take it you coming here means you're ready to discuss what you're looking for?"

She gave a small nod. "Yes, but also I wanted to know what information our kidnapper shared. I'm afraid I'm at a loss as to why they wanted to take me."

"Are you?" A single blond eyebrow arched, and Drag's stormy gray gaze was anything but kind. She'd seen similar keen gazes from her father. People in power often had to second-guess everyone around them and no doubt Drag had adopted a similar habit for a reason.

"I have my own ideas as to why, but—"

"Then share them, because I'd like to know a bit of this story since your presence here may affect not just Hemi, but all of us."

Okay, he has a point. There was a twinge of guilt threading its way through her veins. She'd been determined not to broadcast her past in the hope it would keep the folks of Frog Lick in a spot of ignorance.

Her father wouldn't punish people who had no clue she was even there, right?

"Telling you might put everyone in danger."

"As opposed to not telling us? You assume the people seeking you would believe Full Throttle to be full of ignorant fools?"

"I was hoping to spin things that way if it came down to it." No sense in lying.

Drag crossed his arms, the metal of his cybernetic one drawing her attention. The metal itself wasn't sleek, not like Hemi's. This had been from the first batch. The appendage was a set of small plates woven together like patchwork, but slightly more interlocked, so from a mere glance, they were seamless.

"I'd prefer to be given insight to appropriately plan. Never mistake our acting ability here in Frog Lick."

"Fine...I'm the daughter of Papal, leader of Aurestral. I came here because of Hemi. He was my friend and he offered me an opportunity to avoid being forced to marry someone I don't even know by staying here in Frog Lick. That cover what you thought?"

"Who were you engaged to before you married Hemi?"

"Caden from Osprerine."

"Fuck." Drag stomped off then, before stopping in front of a big sheet of refined Marsanium leaning against a ship frame, and letting his fist fly. The cybernetic marvel let go of two, no three, punches and damn near put a hole through the three-inch-thick piece of metal.

Sophia wished she could pour her frustration out with a violent outburst, but as a woman, she had to keep such desires contained. Her eruptions were more subtle and longer-lasting. *Like running away and marrying someone who your father doesn't approve of.*

Drag took a deep breath then walked back to her. "I don't appreciate our gang being used as a staging ground for some battle with two gangs I have no interaction with. I also want it known that escape from one's obligations doesn't always go the way you think it will. You're being a bit childish."

She clenched her fists. "That's low, and it's not about running from my family. It's about taking what I want and figuring out to have both things I've desired for so long."

"Is one of those things Hemi?" Drag's question speared her because he was the first beside Teija to guess her real reason for coming.

"Do you think me weak if I say yes?"

"Only a fool would think desire makes a person weak. But lust and want can blind someone to a person's genuine nature. Make them think they have a chance at something wonderful and grand until that blindfold is ripped off and they're left to face the Mars sun with nothing but once-hads."

The words were cryptic, steeped in some deep emotion with Drag looking out past Sophia toward the ship bay doors as if caught in some memory replay that only he could see.

"I've wanted him since the day I met him." She chose to be brutally honest with this man because maybe he'd help her...or maybe he'd understand such a bone-deep longing that couldn't be cured by merely forgetting memories.

"But how long have you wanted to rule Aurestral?"

"How did you know?"

Drag smiled, the grin making him appear even more arrogant. "It's not hard to figure. Outside of Frog Lick, women aren't treated with the greatest respect. I know Papal has no male offspring, only the single daughter. Though I never knew her name. He'd have to marry you off, but why settle for a mere mechanic or driver...not when he could try to forge alliances? Though typically, you don't need alliances unless you're already weak, unable to defend yourself."

A master strategist. "Do you really spend this much time thinking through things?"

"Not always, but since the blindfold came off, yes." Drag turned and motioned for her to follow him. "Come, let's talk more of this with our prisoner. And, maybe you might tell me what woes your father suffers from."

"Why would you help me?" There was nothing altruistic about people on Mars. Everyone wanted something. Favors came with debts, and in some cases, losing far more than someone ever wanted to give.

"Because I believe we might be able to help each other, and I owe Hemi a debt. If helping you helps him, then it's worth the trouble."

Chapter Thirteen

Hemi lifted, squatted, punched and pulled his way through over an hour and a half of exercises. He was dripping sweat by the time he was done, but not once had he collapsed from the weight or found himself unable to keep going.

Sophia's belief in him acted as a pivotal driving force to keep pushing. For multiple reasons, the main one being he didn't want to let her down, and the other having to do with a lower part of his anatomy.

He'd been hard as a rock when they'd stopped kissing. His cock was primed for a good time and Hemi still found himself shocked at what Sophia's touch had done to him. *Because you never expected to get aroused again.*

Not for a lack of trying, but nothing had happened. Another thing he'd lost to the explosion, a part of his life gone forever. Sophia had proved that wasn't the case, but overheating... Hell, he dabbed himself with a towel and didn't feel hot at the moment.

In fact, he felt closer to the person he'd been before the wreck than the alien that had been born after.

"We need to talk." The words came with the opening and slamming of the door to his workout room. Snapper approached, steps firm and hard. The frown on his face matched the displeasure Hemi had already experienced over the last couple days, though he hadn't run into Snapper since announcing Jack was gone.

"About?" Hemi intentionally lifted two tire rims, flexing the muscles on his arms. Intimidation was probably moot where Snapper was concerned. Between him and Drag, the former was built like his entire body had been honed in a fire. Though lifting engine blocks on a continual basis tended to tone a man well.

"The fact you were hiding the Aurestral princess under our noses. First Jack and now this. We're already at near breaking point. Did you ever think — "

Hemi dropped the rims, the metal pieces thudding against the ground, effectively silencing Snapper for a moment. "Think? That's all I do. You really want to go there? I was helping a friend. It didn't seem important to share details that might draw attention to her. Jack needed that push too. He cares for Shannon and was going to leave her alone and fighting."

"For a guy who wants to help others, you certainly can't stand receiving any help yourself." Snapper's voice was low, a vibration of anger threaded into those words. He'd offered Hemi help since day one of him waking up. To train, to assist in any way and Hemi had told him to screw off, the same with Drag and Jack.

He didn't need them... *No, not after what they did to me.*

"That's different."

"Speak it or die angry but quit hiding your feelings from everyone."

Hemi crouched down, standing the tire rim on end and rolling it toward him. His gaze locked on the dullness of the metal, starting to corrode from the red dirt it got left on repeatedly. In some ways, he was like the rim, his shine fading away.

"You did this to me. You, Drag and Gina turned me into this freak of nature. Like some monster from an old Earth story. I'm barely half-human and that half can't keep up with the rest. I'm doing all this strength training to help myself adapt but I may never be able to be me again. Then the problem with the nanites — "

"No, don't go blaming shit on us for that. We didn't know and you let Jack walk out of here before Gina could give him clearance or extract what was needed to fix us all." Snapper approached him now, then crouched in front of him, the tire rim the only thing keeping them apart.

"I don't regret for a second saving you. You deserved to be saved. I know you don't think you're much now and you're trying to do a good deed here and there to somehow fill the emptiness, but you're missing the point. Drag, Jack and I…we know how you feel. Sure, you have more cybernetic parts than we do, but we've been in the situation of bodies adjusting. Sweating through the nights, unsure if our hearts would pound out of our chests or if we'd overheat and fall down. This isn't new."

Hemi lifted his head, looking Snapper head on. "You never told me that before?"

"You never fucking asked. Just buried your head in the damn red dirt and treated us all like assholes who used and abused you."

"Didn't you? My opinion was never sought."

"Sorry that we didn't think to ask you while you were passed out from the never-ending nerve pain with your body being burned to hell. These were split-second decisions, ones we agreed we'd pay the cost for and if you think we're not paying, we are."

"Not the way I am."

Snapper reached for the tire rim, yanking it out of Hemi's hands as he stood, then threw it across the room with a roar. "We're paying because we've lost you regardless. This conversation is proof enough. You hate us for saving you and we hate ourselves for letting the damn accident happen to begin with."

Hemi pushed himself up. "Then we're mutually upset."

"Yeah, but what do you plan to do about it?"

Would he leave? Would he stay and try to race again? What about Sophia and their marriage... *What marriage? You're broken and all the desire in the world won't stop your heart from giving up when you try to fuck her.*

The depressing thought ignited his anger all over again. "You'll have to wait for the surprise like everyone else."

Snapper ground his teeth and glanced around as if looking for another inanimate object to deploy violence onto. Instead, he took a few deep breaths. "Fine. Just meet us at the mechanics bay after dinner. We need to chat."

"Who's ordering it?"

"Drag, who the hell else?" Snapper turned on his heel and stomped off.

Hemi couldn't concentrate after Snapper left and opted to return to his house for a shower to get cleaned up. Except that didn't help much either because Sophia's scent was all over the place. She'd permeated his home, even his bed. He'd find no peace here anymore either.

Their closeness from this morning and the connection they'd shared seemed so far away. He needed to get lost, to stop thinking and turn everything off.

That might have been how he found himself reaching for his semi-erect cock and stroking away as he stood within the ion shower. With his cybernetic hand bracing the wall in front of him, he replayed how Sophia's lips had tasted, the way she'd breathe in short pants. How her body had been flush against his, her breasts soft and perfect. He wanted her beneath him, whispering his name sharply.

His heartbeat picked up and his skin felt hot. He refused to open his eyes, instead chasing this dangerous possibility. If he could survive this and find completion, then maybe. Increasing the friction, he kept his thoughts on Sophia, on the look in her eyes, that pure lust and adoration. The way she'd wanted more from him, how she'd cupped his cock and stroked him. There were so many possibilities.

He tried to envision his fingers playing with her nipples. Sinking into her wet heat as she worked his shaft with her hand. Her touch would be soft, her pleasure acute. He could imagine her little moans and gasps. He'd please her with his hand first then his mouth. Tongue her until she writhed beneath him...when she bucked against him in desperation.

His skin felt like it was on fire, burning, and it hurt. *Hell, it hurts so much. Damn.*

He released his cock like it was fire branded. Leaning into the wall with his cybernetic shoulder, he stood still and let the ions swirl around him as his heartbeat slowed. The blood pounding in his ears faded to a dull sensation. He'd been close.

A glance down — his cock was still rock solid, unable to be remedied.

I can't let her touch me.

Funny situation he found himself in. No way could they complete the act. He'd be limited to pleasuring her. *Will that be too much?*

He hit his fist against the wall, ignoring the crack the impact made. There was no way to test the theory without Sophia. What if he let her down? *Damn, it would be embarrassing.* Here he'd told her they would go slow and he was the one pushing, rushing…chasing this idea that he needed to be more for her because otherwise he was nothing.

The bell rang throughout Frog Lick, signaling the end to another workday. That was his cue. Time to face this uncertain future and how much time he'd get with her before he was pulled away to deal with Drag and their concerns.

* * * *

Sophia had been at the Watering Hole bar for the last hour watching Gaia and the smooth way she worked the crowd. Whether feeding or watering, she made sure everyone was cared for in a fashion that made it seem personable. She asked questions, details.

Drag had told Sophia that the true force behind Frog Lick was Gaia, a woman who didn't know a stranger. Once they were in her purview, she took care of a person unless she found a reason to distrust their motives.

The Full Throttle leader had suggested that Sophia learn the inner workings and tricks to anticipating needs, understanding the people around her, from Gaia. This was after he'd refused to let her talk to her captured kidnapper. Drag had stated emphatically that the man from a gang-town known as Skeiron would be released back to his people soon enough. That she didn't need to worry about their motives.

She'd inquired if he'd figured out who hired them and Drag had been non-committal, merely stating that it wasn't her parents, so no worries there. Of course, he recommended that she reach out to her parents first instead of them finding out from her bodyguard or another messenger.

"I can't risk a war. Not when I'm still trying to find a way to fight back against the gang that hurt Hemi."

As much as she despised being dismissed, she'd remembered Hemi's words of advice and how Drag was ultimately in charge. So, she'd silenced her concerns and focused more on her other reasons for being here. How she wanted to effect change for her future and the future of Aurestral, similar to what Drag had done for Frog Lick. There would be no differences between a group of haves and have nots.

"Here you are. One glass of recycle. Though the house brew is probably better."

Sophia took the glass and swallowed a sip. "Thanks, Gaia. This hits the spot."

"Let me know if you need anything else."

"I do have one question. How do you remember everyone's names? Even me, a new person, you didn't forget."

Gaia grinned at her. "Drag send you here?"

She wasn't the first one to come to Gaia for advice. "Would you be mad if I said he did?"

"No, I'm glad you came anyway because Petal and I were worried. You got taken and we weren't able to do much except alert folk for help. I'm sorry. I don't want you to think we abandoned you."

The concern on Gaia's face revealed the faint lines around the woman's eyes...gray eyes that were piercing and provoking.

"You did all that you could and Hemi and Drag came and saved me. Better than not doing anything. I don't blame you at all for what happened." She leaned up on the bar. "But if you still feel bad, you can make it up to me by showing me how you run your business."

Gaia chuckled and tucked a flyaway hair behind her ear. "Sure thing. The first part you asked about remembering...when they introduce themselves, assign their name to a feature or part of the information they share. It's Petal, who works in airponics and has curly hair. Three times, I repeat each set of information three times. People are simple, but nothing inspires appreciation so much as common courtesy and consideration. All too often those at the top of the food chain forget that their positions are meant to support those around them, not degrade. I'll be back later, but if I get busy or you need to leave, just swing by tomorrow after the bell."

Sophia nodded in thanks and took another drink as those words tumbled over in her head. Consideration for others...her father said similar things but said it in a way that implied all that he did was already part of his thought for those of Aurestral. *Even as people starve.*

Her planned fiancé's father had similar beliefs, that being in charge somehow made them above conflicting opinions or admonishment when things were going well. They knew what was best, when in fact, if Frog Lick proved anything, it was that her gang and others were anything but the greatest.

"I take it you didn't get the answers you were looking for today, if the way you're staring into that glass of recycle means anything."

Her head snapped up, gaze colliding with Hemi's golden one. Those eyes were filled with mirth, admiration and desire. Heavens were less beautiful than the way Hemi looked at her now and she'd wished for this day for so long.

All previous concerns about leadership, loyalty and musings of confusion faded at his appearance. She only wanted one thing, to grab him and hold him against her. To kiss those plump lips of his and taste him again.

"I don't need any answers when I've got you."

A faint pink filled his cheeks, and she reached for him, spreading her palm over the heat blossoming on his skin.

"Then I can't interest you in dinner first?"

"I'm starving, but not for food."

He reached up, grabbed her hand and laced his fingers between hers. "Then let's go."

Chapter Fourteen

Sophia went willingly with Hemi guiding them out of the Watering Hole. Though instead of heading in the direction of his home, he walked toward the mechanics bay.

"Where are we going?"

"To spend some time under the stars." They circled around to the side of the building where a metal ladder was affixed to the wall.

He stopped underneath it and guided her hand to the first rung. "Climb up first and I'll follow."

"Are you sure this is okay?"

He grinned, and in the awakening evening hours with the sky a dark shade of purple, minutes away from night, she could see the excitement in his eyes. "It will be like old times."

Turning toward the ladder, she started to climb and recalled the first time she'd attempted to scale a building. Hemi had been with her then, inspiring her to move quick, but mainly to hide from a merchant's sons who were after them for giving away food to starving kids.

Her rebellious nature would have been almost squashed by fear if not for Hemi. Now she climbed, her chest heavy with the same emotion then. Excitement, temptation of the forbidden, because were they even allowed to be up there?

When she reached the top and climbed onto the roof itself, she didn't miss the clear bubbles carving out certain areas of the rooftop—sky lights designed to let natural light filter into the bay. She carefully navigated between them, then she saw the blanket laid out with a small lantern and a basket with a few food items.

"Hemi?"

He interlocked his hand with hers once more and guided her forward. "A nice evening among the stars. A chance to reconnect. This is us taking things slow."

She'd forgotten about the lengthy progress he wanted, so caught up in the way he looked at her that she'd momentarily believed everything was fine. Physical connection could hurt him, but with his eagerness, she'd believed he'd found an alternative. A way for them to be together.

"You're not happy?" He'd glanced at her, and she quickly shook her head, willing away the frown she wore.

"No, that's not it at all. This is amazing. I'm just reminded of what we've lost so many years apart."

He gave her a gentle squeeze, then pulled her with him as he sat down on the blanket. The basket contained a bottle of brew, a couple glasses, a couple random fresh fruits or vegetables, she wasn't sure which, and some bread.

"It's not a hot meal, but figured you'd like a little something."

"What is everything?"

"The brew is made with citrus fruits. It's a bit different than normal, but I remember how you liked the blood oranges your parents imported from Io." He opened the bottle and poured a glass for her.

"The bread is pre-sliced and it's a rye bread, there's a sour bite to it, but when you pair with the sweetness of the Haven pears, a soft fruit, the flavors balance each other. Remember that time we snuck those savory pastries, but you couldn't eat the one without a berry or two? You loved the mixture of sour and sweet."

She took a piece of the bread with a slice of pear on top. "How do you even remember all of these things?"

Of course, she chose to bite into the morsel before he answered. The pairing was as delicious as he'd described, and it burst over her tongue. The sweet, the sour...a hint of bitter. *There is something marvelous in eating food selected especially for you.*

Sophia dared to look in his eyes, as she finished her bite. There she saw desire and fondness shining back at her.

"I remember every little adventure we had. All the ones you took against your parents' wishes because I inevitably paid for them with chores or punishment."

"Hemi, you never said —"

"I don't regret it. The joy you gave me in our running through Aurestral, playing heroes that would take from the rich and give to the deserving, exploring the alleys and hidden nooks, marking up walls with color to inspire... Each one made me part of who I am and helped give me the courage to leave and explore beyond what the gang-town could offer."

There were words he wasn't saying, parts he left out. She could only imagine what he'd gone through in retribution for disobeying when she would drag him away on a so-called adventure.

"I appreciate that, but you're leaving out the part where I badgered you until you came with me. All those penances you paid were really meant for me. I'm surprised you still want anything to do with me."

He'd called his offering little, but it meant the world to her. Sophia had been given everything in life, from the moment she'd been born, but those things were always considered her due by her parents. They weren't done out of caring or concern — even consideration for whether she liked something or not was thrown to the wayside in favor of what was best.

Hemi's confession made her realize she had treated others and their time and possessions the same way. Even in the face of their past, with her poor treatment of him and with his limited means, he'd gone out of his way to find things she liked, to remember what she enjoyed.

"Are you crying?"

Her vision had blurred, but she hadn't noticed at first. She reached up to touch her cheek and her fingertips met water.

"It's been a couple of crazy days. A crazy week. I'm just a little tired." She swiped at her face, willing herself to stop showing so much emotion. The last thing she'd wanted when Hemi brought her up here was to become a blubbering mess. Her plan revolved around being sensual and sexy, amping them back up to where they had been earlier in the day.

"It's okay if you are. Showing how you feel isn't a bad thing. Neither is talking."

Yet confronting those feelings only compounded her guilt. She needed to explore her previous actions and misconceptions about how to treat people, even Hemi, but she didn't want to lose the momentum they'd gained prior.

She leaned in close to him and slid a hand along his thigh. The cybernetic one was fully covered, but she loved the strength his replacement limbs conveyed.

"What if I don't feel like talking?"

This was what Hemi had feared, Sophia not content with discussion, with evaluating what they used to be to each other. He understood her desire to take things to the next step, but the risk to him was a little too great to attempt.

Not to mention, while he'd always cared for her, putting himself out in this way was such a huge risk. Especially when he was unsure of his future.

He gently removed her hand, hating the frown that appeared on her face. "It's too risky for me. I know it's easier to get lost in the physical and if you were throwing yourself at me prior to the accident, I wouldn't hesitate. Also, I like your forwardness, but right now…"

Did he want to explore all the old wounds along with his feelings toward her? She'd scratched at a sore spot he hadn't realized existed when she mentioned her guilt about being the reason he'd suffered so much.

He'd become a victim of her wants and desires, but not in a way that benefited him. Even now, this marriage…he'd set up himself to play the sacrifice because would she really be hurt from this when she was forced to return home? Hemi had wanted to be a good friend, a hero, to embody some of the traits he'd loved about the folks of Full Throttle this entire time, but that might not have been a wise choice.

"You'd rather talk?" She fidgeted with a fraying piece of the straw on the basket edge and he glanced between her movements and the expressive reluctance on her face. "Even when you and both know exploring the past isn't going to do us any good."

"What if it did? You talk about changing, being a better leader. I want to figure out where to go, what to be with this new body. Why not do that together?"

The frown on her face deepened, grooves indenting in her skin around her eyebrows. "You could have everything, all of me, and that's what you're asking for?"

To anyone else's ears, it might have seemed silly, but he'd grown since his near-death experience. The mere physical wasn't the only desire on his mind. The future life he wanted would involve trying to find a way to be more than a mere driver who got his rocks off with high speeds and fast living.

This wouldn't last forever, of that he was sure, but damn if he wouldn't get something out of this time with Sophia before she left. He'd take healing the wounds of his past.

"Yeah, it is."

She shook her head and chuckled. "Never thought I would be the one begging you to touch me."

All right, I'm a liar. Because he wanted something physical. "You don't need to. Ask me."

"If I say I'm willing to talk, will you touch me in return? I get you can't physically penetrate me without it causing some issues, but your fingers could."

Hemi coughed. "You're saying you want me to finger-fuck you?"

"Yes." She licked her lips and Hemi needed to take a couple calming breaths before he could respond.

His cheeks heated a bit at her words. She sure knew how to fire a man up in under five seconds. Though she surprised him, the fact that she could articulate what she wanted, no hesitation, was a skill he'd always admired. Her forthright nature didn't just exist in her everyday activities but also in her bedroom preferences.

We should be talking, but damn if I can tell her no. "Then scoot closer and unbuckle your pants." His little cock yank in the shower earlier had left him unfulfilled and maybe this could satisfy him for a minute.

She did as he commanded. Her following his commands was almost as arousing as watching her shimmy across the blanket to the spot he'd indicated between his legs and the way she unsnapped her pants and spread the two sides wide to provide access for him.

Leaning her head back against his chest, he absorbed the feel of her against him. Her pulse pounded, her body shivered a bit and she appeared a little restless as she rested her hands atop his thighs.

He'd been with plenty of women and even a couple men. Those situations, he'd been secure in his carnal knowledge or at least solid in the belief that he could do nothing that wouldn't add to the pleasure of the situation.

With Sophia, she was like a new racer he'd never driven. Unknown and unpredictable with no way to tell how she'd handle. He feared he might break or destroy the precious parts that made her a marvel to begin with.

He reached for her hair first, lifting the soft blonde tresses from behind her and draping them over her shoulder. This gave him a better view of her body, the quick rise and compress of her chest. "Are you nervous?"

She let out a little half-laugh. "No, I'm highly aroused, almost to the point of pain. You don't know how long I've wanted this. Today feels like one giant lesson in edging."

"Edging?" He hadn't heard the term before.

"One of my lovers, not long ago, loved to bring me to the brink of orgasm then pull away. Over and over, they'd have me flying toward the atmosphere of sensual bliss only to make me wait. Does that get you off too?"

He could imagine her, in near throes of ecstasy, thrashing against bed sheets with him working her pussy with his tongue and fingers. But he realized then he wouldn't be able to stop until she came because that was what he wanted to see. He didn't want control of her orgasm—he wanted to see her in utter rapture, again and again.

The image spurred him on, and he placed his human hand over her belly. She let out a soft gasp. This was a lesson itself in anticipation and how slow movement could heighten every sensation.

"This isn't edging, it's foreplay." He leaned in and whispered in her ear as his hand reached the waistband of her panties. "And know this. I'll never stop you from coming."

He didn't realize his breathing had become labored as well until he came in contact with the sweet flesh beneath her underwear. Running his fingers over her plump pussy lips, between them, he dipped himself in her wetness. *A fucking dream from true.*

The temptation to push further, to tell her to strip and ride his face, was so damn strong. He settled for bringing those same fingers to his lips. His cock throbbed when she whimpered.

"You don't like it when I pull away? Want me touching that sweet pussy of yours forever?"

She gave a single nod.

"You taste so good. Imagine if I used my tongue instead. I'd lick you clean. Suck your clit till you scream." Hemi moved with his words, touching her clit, dipping lower and circling her entrance, loving how she coated him.

Her pants were more defined now, between little shuttering intakes of breath. She gripped his thighs tightly.

"Fuck me with them, please?"

Already his temperature was rising. Sweat coated his back even in the chilly night air. He dared to dip two fingers into her silken heat and the way her pussy clenched him tight made his cock throb. "I don't think I can for long."

"What about your other fingers?"

The cybernetic metal that wouldn't allow him to feel…hell, he didn't want to be blind to the sensation. Then again, he'd be shielded from physical contact.

"I don't want to hurt you."

She turned her head and pressed a quick kiss to his lips, then a longer one, tracing the seam with her tongue. When she pulled away, she let out a satisfied hum. "Love how I can taste myself on you. You won't hurt me. But I need this, Hemi. What better way to test your stamina? Make me come twice. I bet you can."

Would it be worth it? *Fuck yeah.*

He swapped hands, once again licking his fingers and loving her taste. Then he let his cybernetic counterparts get to work. He was in control — he could easily command his hand to work how he wanted.

Sophia gasped as he pinched her clit. "Yes, lower."

He did as asked, inserting two fingers into her, and pumping them in and out slowly at first. His thumb circled her clit and he worked her for several minutes, increasing the pace as she commanded. While the sensations were almost non-existent, he could still feel when her walls tightened.

She started to squirm against him, pushing her back toward him, then grinding down hard on his fingers. "I need more."

He banded his human arm across her chest and found himself filled with the desire to give her whatever she asked for. "Then you're going to need to hold still, otherwise I can't fuck you the way you want. Now, bear down with that pussy, clench around my fingers. You're coming for me."

The words shocked him, wherever they came from, but he promised to deliver, thrusting up inside her repeatedly, faster than he'd thought himself capable of. With speed, the curve of his fingers and his near constant massage of her clit, she was a moaning mess within minutes. She tried to fight his hold on her, but out of a natural reaction to the fact she wanted to move.

Next time he'd take her in a bed, let her move as much as she wanted.

"I'm going to…" She cut off as her mouth opened wide, but a silent scream emerged. He couldn't feel her release, not with his cybernetic hand. Though the rapture on her face…the sheer blissful look and the way she began to pant again as he refused to let up were glorious. Hemi continued to move his fingers, loving how she shivered beneath him then immediately came again.

Only then did he reduce his pace, and gently pull his fingers out of her. He was going to lick them, but she beat him to it. There was something extremely arousing about watching her clean her own orgasm from his fingers. The lack of sensation on his part didn't dull the eroticism of her actions.

"I could have taken care of that."

She let go of his hand then angled herself so she could kiss him again. He released his hold on her. Open mouths, tongues, like racers competing on a track, but in this case, they were in perfect sync. When she finally pulled back, she grinned. "I figured we could share."

"You're fucking amazing. You know that, right?"

She smiled at him, the brightness in her eyes, the flush to her cheeks. He'd almost say she appeared well-fucked and Hemi could be proud that he'd given her such a look.

"So are you. Turns out those cybernetic parts are good for something. I like the way you finger-fucked me."

"Damn it, Sophia. You're going to make me take you again."

"I wouldn't mind. Though a bed might be more comfortable."

"*Mechanics bay, meeting in five. Hemi, that includes you, so get off the damn roof.*"

"Shit."

Sophia leaned away. "What? Did I say something wrong?"

"No, I just…there's a meeting in the bay below us in five. If they need me, it probably has to do with Jack." Hemi scooted away from Sophia then stood. It was quick work to put the area to rights and Sophia re-snapped her pants and helped.

They folded the blanket and tucked everything into the basket, then she picked up the lantern. He could tell the way her gaze stayed on the items she had something she wasn't saying.

"Go ahead and tell me what's on your mind."

She kicked a small stone across the roof, and it came to a halt against the metal rim of one of the skylights. "How did you forget a meeting until right now?"

Fuck… Explaining the weird connection relay that Gina could use with the cybernetic systems to send messages when they were in close proximity wasn't easy. "I just heard about it when I told you."

"How—"

"I'll have to explain later. Let me help you down from the roof with all this stuff first."

They moved toward the ladder and she shook her head. "You won't have time."

Their descent from the mechanics bay roof was punctuated with a silence that killed the high of their connection moments prior. Though his commitment to Full Throttle had to come first. For multiple reasons.

Reaching the ground, he turned to face Sophia. "I don't want to cut this short, but—"

"Responsibilities are important, and you have some to your gang. It's okay. I'm not hurt by it, but hoping at some point you'll trust me with all your secrets." She leaned into him and instead of kissing him as he'd hoped, she gently eased the basket from his hand.

"Take care of what you need to, and I'll see you after...at home."

The word home from her lips seemed foreign and had his shoulders tensing. He'd never thought of Frog Lick or his place as home. Just a temporary stop on his journey, and after the accident even more so.

He swallowed against the lump in his throat, unable to do more than give her a nod before he decided to walk away first, heading for the mechanics bay door. Their moment on the roof was meant to bring them closer and somehow, he found himself in even more turmoil than he'd started with.

Hemi clenched his jaw and walked as tall and proud as he could, because deep down anxiety was taking root, spreading through him like NiteOx mix meeting sludge. But he had no idea how big the explosion would be.

Chapter Fifteen

"We're down to the wire. Jack isn't back yet, and we must make the decision. There's two weeks until the regional race. If you're not ready, Hemi, we need to know now."

Hemi glanced around the room. Drag leaned against the bed of a hauler. Snapper and Gina were standing near his office door, Snapper's arms wrapped around Gina as if the close contact wasn't just natural but necessary.

Hemi briefly considered if he looked the same way with Sophia or if he could ever leave her with such a content expression on her face. Because Gina seemed completely relaxed even as Full Throttle was on the verge of being utterly screwed.

"Can I take a day to think about it?"

Drag threw a wrench across the room, the metal piece bouncing and echoing off the walls. "Yes, that's fine."

"Tell me how you really feel?" Hemi replied with a half-hearted chuckle, then he saw her. The curly brown hair was a dead giveaway…her bandaged hands, torn pants at the thighs and knees, dirt marring her face and the sun goggles on the top of her head…

Shannon.

Hemi crossed over to Drag and nudged him with his toe then his cybernetic arm. Their fearless leader scowled at him, then he angled his head toward the door, just as Snapper seemed to catch on.

"Where's Jack?" the lead mechanic called out.

"He's been taken."

Turned out Hemi's anxiety was well-deserved. "Fuck."

Drag patted Hemi on the shoulder. Whatever frustrations had existed a minute ago were no longer. Not with this new problem on their doorstep.

As Hemi turned, he saw Gina headed toward Shannon. He tensed, ready to charge forward and separate the two, but the AI surprised him by wrapping Shannon up in a hug.

Gina leaned in close and whispered something in Shannon's ear. The words were enough to spawn tears. Her voice cracked as she replied loudly, "I'm fine, but Jack…Bridget took him."

The AI seemed to hold onto Shannon even more, offering support. "We thought something went wrong when he didn't return with you. We've been discussing options. Now you're here and we have answers. You must have been frightened."

Hemi was super confused. What options? He'd been left out of the loop, and he glanced at Drag, who shook his head, a firm set to his lips. That was the *'not right now'* response. If Hemi was being left out of even more conversations, then why the hell was he even here?

Shannon's voice echoed in the room, her frustration clear. "I'm not frightened. I'm angry and I want to get Jack back. He shouldn't have to pay for my mistakes."

Hemi flipped back toward the women, watching close as Gina pulled away, then stepped back. "You love him?"

Love? Was that important... Shannon had mentioned mistakes.

"What's that got to do with it?" Snapper marched toward them. "Bridget's crazy. He could already be dead."

There was a lot Snapper was leaving out, like how Bridget was his half-sister. She'd been the reason both Snapper and Drag had cybernetic arms to begin with. The fact they'd left Macintosh, once lauded as the gang's best driver and mechanic, to find a place in Frog Lick back when the Smiths still ran the gang spoke volumes to how insane Bridget was.

"No," Drag replied. "She wouldn't kill him. That would guarantee she'd never get what she wants."

Hemi was so damn confused. It was like he'd somehow missed multiple conversations during the last month, and maybe he had. He'd been so locked into his own suffering and recovery...add in Sophia's arrival and their marriage. Maybe he needed to get more involved.

"What does she want?" Hemi asked.

Shannon sighed and linked her hands together. "The plans to your racer. She purposely cheated in a game of cards against me, so I'd be in her debt. The explosion in Hemi's racer wasn't an accident. At least I don't think it was, because she waited to claim what I owed her until I was contacted by Gina's friend on the moonie base. I don't know what she has against you all, but she's bound and determined to defeat you at any cost."

The heaviness in his chest grew. They'd been played from the get-go. Shannon had come here not to help him, but herself. Hemi had been completely suckered. He had believed Shannon to be a common spirit to him. Someone fiercely independent, following their own path, though he hadn't expected her to be big on betrayal. Not when Jack fell for her, like Hemi almost had. No lying about it, he was attracted to her, but when Sophia showed up, he couldn't deny what he really wanted was the woman he'd grown up with.

Hemi noticed Snapper glance at Drag and anger rushed hot and fresh, coating whatever hurt he carried with another layer. He'd been left out of information shared between those two. They considered him a 'brother' but the connection didn't run very deep when they failed to involve him beyond wondering if he'd drive their damn racer.

Shannon stood firm. "Whatever her reasons, I don't really give a shit. But I'm willing to do whatever to get Jack back. If it was as simple as trading myself for him, I would. Though I'm afraid she won't accept that as a decent trade anymore."

"No, she won't. Bridget has committed to kidnapping one of ours instead of using an outside source. Are you sure it was her?" This was from Drag, who walked over to Shannon as she tugged a crumbled piece of paper from her pocket and shoved her fist toward Drag. He picked up the ball from her hand with his cybernetic one.

Unfolding the letter, Drag's eyes traced the words and Hemi watched as the frown on Drag's face deepened, a sharp indent above his left eye, his gaze narrowing. He shoved the letter at Snapper, who let out a string of curse words after he read the contents. Hemi was next to receive the letter.

We have Jack, and we're not giving him back until I see those racer plans. Bring them within the week or we start cutting his fingers off...

"We go after him," Drag declared.

Snapper announced his agreement and without a second thought, Hemi joined in. "Agree."

Because he'd foolishly encouraged Jack to chase after love, to chase after the dream of a connection with Shannon who might have been playing them all along.

"For more than one reason," Gina replied. "The blood Jack left wasn't enough. I can't replicate the nanites without more, unfortunately. If we leave out our emotional attachments to him, he's still needed to ensure the rest of you with cybernetics survive."

Gina wasn't wrong and Hemi would need to be whole if he had a tiny chance of leaving here without the need to return.

Shannon frowned and crossed her arms. "He has to be worth more than blood to you."

Gina waved away her concern. "Yes, he is. Still, it bears mentioning we need to bring him back alive and intact."

A bang, heavy and resounding, could be heard against the main bay doors. Then it was repeated twice more, the signature knock signaling the message was urgent and important.

Snapper went to answer it. His booming voice barked out a muffled greeting of some sort. When he returned, his face was flustered, his cybernetic hand clenched tight while the other one held a cloth. "You're right, she's desperate."

Snapper handed over the cloth and a small card to Drag, who peeled back the stained linen to reveal a small finger, darkened and decaying.

" 'This is your first present, two more days and I'll send another'," Drag read aloud before crumpling the card up in his hand and tossing it. "She's determined to take pieces from all of us... I'm not letting her get another one."

Shannon stared at the pinky and put a fist against her mouth. "We have to call someone. The protectorate, the commission...someone can stop her."

Hemi wanted to call her out, question her sentiment for Jack. Sure, he'd been aware of her betrayal, but it sat wrong with him. Maybe because of all the memories he'd stirred up, his own past haunting him like a specter.

Instead, he focused on the hard truths. "You know better. Protectorate cares only if the commission is threatened. Commission don't care unless a gang is breaking the rules of the charters. Kidnapping some woman's man and holding him hostage until she pays her debts is perfectly legal in their eyes."

The cruelty of their world meant the only way to save Jack would be to endanger themselves. But he deserved a rescue and more—on that point Hemi could agree. His anger simmered deep with the reminder that the same woman torturing Jack had changed his body forever.

"So, I guess it's best that I go alone." Shannon started to pace back and forth between the door and their little group. "What I'm looking at you for is a bargaining chip. Give me something, even a fake something. I need to go to Bridget with some sort of plan in place."

"You're not going by yourself. That's not how we work." Drag had covered Jack's pinky back up and set it to the side.

"I can't possibly risk harm coming to anyone Jack loves."

Her willingness to sacrifice herself redeemed her a bit and Hemi reached out, placing a hand on her shoulder, stilling her movement. "But you're the one Jack cared about the most. Nothing bad can happen to you, either. Ultimately, Full Throttle's involvement is not your decision to make. We can decide how we want to proceed."

Tears gathered in her eyes and Shannon blinked rapidly as if she were trying to chase them away.

"If she wants to go, maybe we should let her. We all go in ready for a fight, we're just going to start a war." This came from Snapper, who held onto a piece of metal side panel from a hauler, gripping it as if he couldn't decide whether to crush it or throw the damn thing.

Drag shrugged. "Seems like she's wanting a war no matter what. Maybe it's time we give it to her."

"A war?" Hemi hated the idea. "Do you really want to bring that down on Frog Lick now? With the championship still up in the air?"

Of course, his dumbass mouth had to bother mentioning the very big concern that had summoned them all to the mechanics bay in the first place. Had his rendezvous with Sophia really taken place a mere couple solar hours prior?

"Hey, you're one to talk when we could already have answer—"

Gina's giggle cut Snapper off. The AI had a knuckle in her mouth and was staring at the floor.

"Care to share, love?" Snapper asked.

Gina lifted her head, a wide grin on her face. "I have an idea, but it will still be dangerous. If Bridget really has assassins and bullies on her side, any plan could result in someone getting hurt."

"As long as it's not Jack, I'm good," Shannon replied as she fingered the chain around her neck, then gripped the charm hanging from it in her palm.

Hemi didn't like how Gina mentioned people getting hurt. He was already hurt, still recovering, and Drag's statement rang through his head once more. Bridget wanted to take pieces from all of them. Instead, he shoveled that fear down, determined to be of help this time. He might not be able to drive a racer, but he'd do whatever they needed to rescue Jack.

"All right, then this is what we'll do. We follow Shannon's suggestion. Give Bridget a drive, but when she plugs it in, there will be a virus that will shut down their firewalls and let me in. Then I download whatever I can. That will give us an idea of what Bridget's planning, hopefully." Gina interlocked her hands as she continued. "Then we create a distraction, some sort of explosion, and Shannon will have to be the one to get Jack out. That means Snapper, Hemi, you'll both be needed for the distraction part. Posted at one end of Macintosh, while Drag, you play the rescue driver once Shannon gets him out."

"There's a lot of unknowns with this whole plan." Hemi couldn't help but call out the obvious. Gina spoke of distractions and different ends of town... "How do we even know where Jack is being held?"

"We won't without sending Shannon in by herself. She'll have to get inside, and once we spot her entering a building, then we know how to move. There will be pieces that come into play as the situation evolves. With all of us on-site, it's a non-issue. Though there is more risk to Shannon." Gina paused and glanced at the other woman. "You get that, Shannon...you'll be the target."

She nodded. "I'm good with that."

Hemi found himself believing in the conviction behind her words and the fierce determination in her gaze. She might have started out with a goal of betraying them for her own gain, but the trip with Jack had changed her somehow.

He just hoped they weren't too late, because whether he wanted to admit it to himself or not, without Jack, his future was looking more dismal by the minute.

* * * *

Sophia was alone again, frustration her constant companion, even after she'd believed last night had meant things were changing between her and Hemi. The only upside was a note. He'd at least left her one this time.

Away on business. Be back in two solar days tops. Stick to your plan and stay out of trouble.

No platitudes, though, which had her second-guessing the intimacy they'd shared the night before. Sticking to the plan meant meeting up with Gaia and learning more about Frog Lick, about leadership and how they operated this gang without a strict hierarchy elevating Drag above the rest of them.

Better than her and Hemi digging deep into the past between them. If examined too closely, it might make Hemi resent her very presence. *Because you caused this, him running away, having to come here…*

Sure, logically speaking, Hemi had made the decisions on his own, but if Sophia had let him be, the possibilities were endless. He might have stayed in Aurestral, been elevated to driver status, won championships and been considered a worthy partner for her.

Fantasies she could daydream about, but reality lay in front of her. She readjusted her sun goggles and dared to glance up at the sign for the Watering Hole swinging in the breeze. In the harsh light of day, the building itself looked old and weathered. Random swirls of red dust wafted through the air kicked up by the breeze.

Frog Lick didn't have Aurestral's high walls that blocked out the winds, or the domed fans that sat atop their four corners and tallest buildings to filter out the dust and spread cool air across the city.

Time to go inside and occupy her day. Anything to quit wondering about Hemi.

She'd barely made it inside before Gaia was waving her over to the bar.

"Well, you slept in this morning. Late night?"

Sophia didn't feel like confessing how she'd waited up for Hemi, hoping he'd come home and continue more of what they'd started. Even now, her body craved the taste of pleasure and sexual release he'd provided. She selfishly wanted more of that.

Damn it, you're just scratching an itch.

Because what else could there be between them? The future would end as soon as her parents forced the issue of her return. Drag had confirmed yesterday with the captive Skeiron that he was on a revenge mission. Her family hadn't come for her yet.

"Restless sleeping."

Gaia winked at her. "If I had a man like Hemi around, I would probably be a little restless too."

Sophia was halfway onto a stool when Gaia snapped her fingers at her.

"Nope, don't bother sitting. You said you want to know how all this works? That Drag wanted you to have the full experience?"

Sophia gave a small nod with one ass cheek on a stool.

"Good, then follow me. Slide those sun goggles in place. We're going down the road a bit." Gaia walked out from behind the bar, her twin braids swaying as she headed for the exit. Sophia stepped in behind her and paused as Gaia stopped at the main door and called out, "Mels and Tawny, keep an eye out, would you? And serve lunch with only one biscuit. Limited amounts today since the grinder went down."

There was murmuring acknowledgment that Sophia didn't quite catch but seemed to do the trick for Gaia, as the older woman stepped out of the front door, then pulled her goggles in place and a piece of cloth over her mouth before marching out into the sun.

No words were exchanged as the wind had picked up a bit more, swirling red around them. The fine particles were annoying, and Sophia had forgotten to bring a cloth for her face. Further proof she wasn't used to living here. Instead, she had to put her arms over her mouth as they walked. Though her covered forearms failed to provide full protection—dirt particles still gathered across her cheeks and in the corner of her mouth.

She was relieved when they reached their destination, another building about halfway down the main stretch. There were a pair of windows hung with knitted curtains in various colors, closed tight. A sign on the door said "The Frog Lick Social Club." Gaia knocked in some sort of tapping pattern with her knuckles. A single tap came, then a lock slid and the door opened.

Gaia reached for her, urging Sophia forward into the dark room ahead of them. Sophia hesitated, because what if this was another trap? Trust wasn't won easily and Drag's offer to have Gaia show her the ropes took on a more ominous meaning.

She was shoved into the room, then Gaia scuffled in behind her, slamming the door shut before throwing the lock.

"You move slower than men in the mines. Gonna let all the dirt in here if we kept the door open any longer."

Sophia tugged off her sun goggles and her eyes began to adjust. A few low-light lamps were placed on various surfaces throughout the room. There were chairs, a table with a tall pitcher filled with a semi-clear liquid and glasses. A few covered platters, hopefully with food.

Sophia's stomach let out a soft growl.

"You're hungry? Good." Gaia stepped around her. "Ladies, I apologize for the delay, but I was waiting on our special guest for today's meeting. Meet Sophia, Hemi's wife."

A small group gathered next to her, and Sophia found herself fidgeting awkwardly with her hands and rocking back and forth from her heels to the tips of her toes. She was a little scared, meeting these women, who, outside of Petal and Gaia, she didn't know.

"Oh, I can't believe you convinced him to bind to you. Seemed like he'd never select someone." This came from an older woman with black and gray hair.

Another lady, a woman with red hair, tapped her on the shoulder twice. "Yuma, it's not nice to say anything other than congratulations. No speculation, leave the woman and her relationship with our driver alone. I'm Artie, by the way."

"Yeah, and she'll screw anything that moves. She tried for Hemi a couple times, but no dice." A brunette with short hair nudged Artie out of the way. "You're some fancy woman from Aurestral, right? All sorts of rumors are spreading about you."

Sophia stood there tongue-tied for a moment, a bit overwhelmed at the commentary being thrown her way. She swallowed hard then found the courage of her voice. "Rumors aren't nearly as much fun as truths, are they? If you let me get a seat over there, I'll answer whatever you want."

"Ooh." Artie slid back in again and looped her arm around Sophia's. "Get out of the way, ladies. I want in on this tell-all because I have one burning question to ask."

The redhead guided Sophia to a chair and she sat down, taking in the small group now huddled around her, chairs scooted in. She wasn't sure if she was going to be the one learning anything today or if these women were going to start trying to pry details about Hemi from her.

"I want to know if it's true there are more single men in Aurestral than any other gang-town on Mars."

Wait, what?

The one called Yuma chuckled. "That's an easy answer, it's true. I want to know about the strip show that's held in the underground nightclub in Aurestral. The one where the male drivers do sexy dances and take off their clothes for Upper clientele. Any way you could sneak a group of us in there?"

There were several small whoops as Petal and Gaia stuck to the outer ring of the group and grinned with knowing smiles. Sophia had expected these ladies to turn against her, interrogate her for being an outsider, demand her reasoning for coming into their town and locking up a bachelor. She certainly didn't plan on them wanting to know more about the gang-town she was from.

"I'm not sure we should be talking about trips into another territory."

"Oh, we definitely should," one of the ladies replied. Sophia couldn't tell who over all the eyes filled with mirth and smiling.

This is so not what I planned for. The experience was like walking into a pit of slithers only to discover fur-buns instead.

Then she remembered what Gaia had mentioned, building rapport with people by relating to them. She'd done her best in Aurestral to keep so many aspects of her life private, secret. Sharing the inner workings of how her father operated and the businesses supported the town was considered betrayal. Except those years of quiet had done nothing but ensure things never changed. She'd been complicit with her silence. Here in Frog Lick she refused to cover for her family any longer. If anything, she needed to make herself relatable so these women would be encouraged to share their knowledge with her, give her ways to change Aurestral's future and escape the clubs and trafficking.

"There is a club, called The Ironworks. And you're right, Yuma…only men work there." A not-so-secret club, as Sophia had discovered today, and one of the few ways her family funneled money into Aurestral. Though they engaged in selling women in different ways.

"Are they all stacked and racked?" Artie bit into her lower lip, eyes staring off somewhere past Sophia, caught in some imaginary idea.

"The Uppers who attend wouldn't want it any other way. There is dancing, nude spectacles and even nights where the men are auctioned off for private shows and pleasures."

A low whistle and a couple purring noises erupted around the women.

"What I wouldn't give to have the flash for that."

"What else? Tell us more."

More? The things she wanted to tell weren't very fun. "There are more orphans than solid homes. Families ripped apart by the club, the female auctions and the never-ending pursuit of crinkle that can't make up for the hungry mouths left in the wake of greed. Those who run the daily workings of our gang are either considered less-than-desirable in some way or children." Those were the memories she held. The times she and Hemi had acted the role of thieves, like some old Earth tale about those who stole from the rich to give to the poor. She'd tried so hard, and each time they had been caught, she'd been ultimately forgiven with minor punishments and Hemi had suffered.

I'm horrible for thinking we didn't have a wider canyon dividing us.

"So, your people suffer too?" This was from Petal, who had moved closer.

"Yes, every day, though it's hard to break them of such a vicious cycle when I have no way to provide for them." She'd tried to give them food, especially those children left behind, though her meager efforts were too far apart and varied to provide any long-lasting impact.

"Without stability, the best crumble and falter," Gaia offered. "This is where Drag met us. All of us were given to vice, to easy ways to get by, but then he encouraged us to take charge and presented opportunities to change things."

Sophia's chest got a little tight at the strength in Gaia's words. She wanted to know more. "How?"

"For us women…by giving us a voice, taking our input and encouraging us to embrace new skills. The airponics bay, gardening. We grow our food. We catch wildlife in traps and use them for protein and all manner of things. You'd be surprised the knowledge we've built, shared from old texts and digital recordings. There is a vast wealth of information not readily provided, but for a price or a trade, the moonies give it up freely."

Sophia marveled at this. "What would be worth a trade to Aurestral?"

"You're asking the right question, but at the wrong time." Gaia moved even closer, weaving between the women sitting and dropping cross-legged onto the floor right in front of her. The woman had a grace to her that would make anyone envious. "Leadership involves thinking about strengths, weaknesses and how you leverage them. Our weakness was our inability to feed ourselves, which in turn led to deeper problems. Once we conquered our stomachs, then the only thing stopping us was greed."

Sophia twirled the idea in her head, and she could see the potential, the blossoming of possibilities. Though getting anyone to follow her would be outlandish. Still, she couldn't give up—this might be a way to the future she wanted. Something more like how daily lives were lived in Full Throttle. Ones where bellies were full, hands were occupied and hearts were content.

"Tell me more."

Chapter Sixteen

Hemi had ignited a sludge depot. So fucking illegal and if they'd been caught...his human side ached, fatigued by all the movement.

Fuck Macintosh.

They were the reason—Bridget especially, as their leader—that he found himself in this position anyway. No sympathy for these bastards who thought the best way to revenge was to blow up a racer with a driver they'd never met.

He readjusted his position in the hauler and did his best to keep his cybernetic arm away from anything it might grip too tight.

"We did it!" This came from Snapper. Gina sat in the passenger seat and Hemi hung out in the back. "Never thought I'd find joy in lighting my old gang-town on fire."

"They deserved it," Hemi mumbled.

The wind whipped by them as they traveled back to Frog Lick. They'd left ahead of Drag, who was in charge as the getaway vehicle for Jack and Shannon. The fire of a flare fifteen minutes after they'd departed at high speeds was the signal that Drag had been successful.

Hemi found himself anxious to get back. He wanted to see Sophia and had been reduced to leaving her a paper message. She'd slept so peacefully, with her little breaths, the slow rise and fall of her chest. Those kind thoughts were replaced rapidly with more erotic ones.

How she'd come from his fingers alone and enjoyed being touched with a part of him that couldn't actually feel. With Jack back and the second-gen nanites available, would it change? *Does it matter?*

"The move was needed, but the fire was a declaration of war." Gina's statement brought with it a fresh new dread.

Hemi didn't want Sophia in harm's way, knowing Bridget had no qualms about killing people. The woman seemed to delight in torture.

"She wants a war, she's got one. We're not going to stop. Drag is officially tired of her bullshit and I'm over it, too. Her little tantrums and desire for revenge are childish. I want nothing to do with my birthright..."

Hemi tuned out as Snapper kept talking. How Hemi bemoaned not being involved in gang business, but at the same time he didn't want to emotionally engage himself anymore. The future involved him leaving, moving on to a new adventure. No more entangling himself with situations he wasn't going to have an input on.

"We still need to plan accordingly. Protect those in Full Throttle from her wrath," Gina said.

Yes, he needed to protect Sophia. At least until things ended. Who knew how much time was left before her parents sent someone for her.

Hemi leaned on his cybernetic side a bit more, trying to alleviate the throbbing pain setting up shop in his human extremities. "There will be plenty of time for plans. How far out are we from Full Throttle?"

Snapper glanced over his shoulder. "Maybe an hour or two. What's the rush?"

"I left without really talking to Sophia."

Gina was the next to give him a look. "You're not going anywhere until I synthesize the nanites from Jack. Lesson learned—I can't trust you all to stick around long enough to get things completed."

Shit. Hemi opened his mouth to argue, but immediately shut it. There was a benefit to following through with Gina's commands. The possible rewards outweighed the pitfalls.

"What are these nanites really going to do for me?"

"With the current state of degradation between Jack, Snapper and Drag, it would appear that you would have more risk because your body contains more of them. If these stabilized all of Jack's degradation and rebuilt his strength, I can only hope they provide equilibrium for you."

The statement filled him with a hope he hadn't really had for months. Optimism was hard to find when he kept falling and was unable to go a day without feeling fatigued. He relaxed amid the hum of the hauler engine and the continued conversation between Snapper and Gina. The remaining travel time passed as if nothing.

They were inside the Full Throttle mechanics bay with Drag's hauler pulling in only a few minutes after they did.

"You almost caught up to us?" Hemi asked.

"You and Jack aren't the only drivers here and I know how to make an engine roar." Drag pulled himself out of the hauler and went around to the other side, opening the door for Jack. "He is pretty worse for the wear here, Gina. Needs our medic."

"I need five minutes, three vials. It won't be any more painful than what he's already experienced."

Shannon clung to Jack, the worry and love in her eyes plain as day. His friend glanced between them and said, "Thanks. For getting me out of the hell-hole. Drag, you and Snapper always said the place was scary and I have to agree."

"Let's get this needle stuff over, Jack. So you can go to the doctor." Shannon was already rolling up a sleeve as Gina moved in with her needle and syringe.

Hemi wasn't scared, but he didn't care to watch. A few minutes later and he dared to look. A bandage was now wrapped around Jack's forearm and elbow.

With the blood taken, Drag immediately stepped in to lead. "Snapper and I will take him to the doctor while you work on the synthesizing, Gina. Take care of Hemi first."

"I'm going with you," Shannon replied, not releasing Jack. Her stubbornness was hilarious as Drag stepped aside and let Snapper and Shannon handle guiding Jack toward the door.

"I can go with them if it will be a while."

"Sit your butt down in this chair, Hemington Finster." Gina slammed a chair against the concrete floor and Hemi slid onto the seat as quietly as he could.

"How do you know my full name?"

"Bridget's records. They are downloading and processing now."

"You can focus on treating me and processing a ridiculous amount of data?"

Gina grinned. "I wouldn't be much of an AI if I sucked at multitasking."

She disappeared into her off-shoot room. It had once been used for storage, but after Hemi's accident and racing win, Snapper had let her turn it into an experiment room for the racers, among other things. One with plenty of scientific equipment and the like.

Hemi wasn't interested in that kind of stuff. He knew how engines worked, could break them down and rebuild them in his sleep. Give him those parts, a chassis, a frame and four wheels and he'd be happy.

Gina was constantly in the pursuit of more, which he guessed made her extra appealing to Snapper. She walked out of the room shaking a little vial of blood and silver mixing together. "It's all ready. I separated the nanites, mixed them with the blood I have stored for you in case of emergency. Now we're ready for the injection."

He was scared. Just a tiny bit. "What if this doesn't work?"

Jack's stumbling when he got out of the car was at the forefront of Hemi's mind.

"Don't compare your situation to what you're seeing around you. This will work. Now, roll up your sleeve and try to relax."

"Assuming you want the fleshy side."

Gina smirked as she plunged the need into the vial to extract the contents. "Don't be a smartass to the person who is about to stick you with something sharp."

"Does that mean you might want to fuck me?" He rolled up his sleeve and Gina was already there.

"All done."

He'd barely felt a thing. "Are you sure?"

"Give it two hours and you should start to see a difference. I recommend returning to your house and lying down."

"All right. Any warning signs I should look out for?"

"Fever, aches, chills, vomiting. If you can't hold any food down, let me know. For right now, just rest and let the nanites do their integration. Then test them out and report back to me tomorrow."

"Test them?"

Gina gave him a wink, then left the room, going back to her little makeshift experimentation closet and shutting the door with a slam. He'd been officially dismissed. There was a bit of disappointment at the lack of some big reveal. Nevertheless, he pushed himself out of the chair and made his way out of the bay and to his house. The sun was sinking, another day gone. They'd driven most of the morning to get to Macintosh and get set up. Their thieving and prisoner escape had them departing with the sun high in the sky.

When he finally reached his house, the one thing he looked forward to was seeing Sophia, except...she wasn't there. Not in the main room area, the bedroom, the bathroom. She'd disappeared.

He sighed in relief at the sight of her bag still in his room, then opted to collapse on the bed. There was nothing sweeter than his bed, besides Sophia's lips on his or her body wrapped around him. He inhaled and caught that floral scent she always wore. It had soaked into his bedsheets and made him miss her all the more.

If he hadn't been given specific directions to rest, he would have chased her down right now and dragged her to bed with him. A comforting thought that he had someone to sleep beside.

His eyes closed, mind playing out this dream of togetherness he found himself loving as much as he hated. Together meant something could be taken from him.

* * * *

"Hey...Hemi. Wake up." The soft feminine tones called to him. She was close — he could smell her. "Hemi. It's time."

He opened his eyes and beautiful blonde hair haloed his face, with Sophia leaning in, her lips inches from his. "Where were you?"

"All over Frog Lick with Gaia, and then the Watering Hole. That's where I saw Drag. He said you were back, and Gina had sent you home. Are you feeling okay?"

He took stock of his body, laying there for a minute. Arms, legs, everything felt...everything felt. "Touch my hand."

She reached for the human one and Hemi shook his head. "No, my cybernetic one. Touch it, please."

"Can't resist if you're going to ask so nicely." She reached for him and interlocked their palms, then fingers.

"I can feel you. There. Your heat, pulse and electrical impulses. Holy shit."

"Hemi, you're scaring me a bit, care to tell me what's going on?"

He released her hand then grabbed her face with both of his and kissed her. The sensations traveling through his dormant limb were a marvel. Her soft lips, her tongue... *Shit, this is getting hot.*

Pulling back, he dared to spread a cybernetic thumb over her lips, loving the way she shuddered at his touch.

"Tell me how that felt."

Her lashes fluttered as he repeated the process. "Like sparks, and then they spread through my body with sensation and arousal. Hemi, I want to do more of what we did on the roof. I'm tired of waiting. Does this new ability change things?"

His cock was already rock hard at her mention of the roof. "I think it might, and I'm willing to try."

"Even after all we talked?"

"It's the past. This is the now. Let's not worry about that and live in this moment. If it makes you feel better, I never blamed you. At least I did my best to remind myself whenever I did that I was the one who agreed. I could've told you no."

"Could you have?" She stroked his cheek with her own hand, up and down. He loved her palm against the stubble on his face.

"Maybe, we won't ever know. But I don't want to say no now."

"Then don't. I want you to take me like you would one of those dust honeys. Use me up until I can't move, and I've come so many times the sheets are soaked."

"You're fucking good at talking dirty." He helped her remove her top, exposing those luscious breasts. This time was better than the last because he finally got to see them. They were here just for him.

He leaned in and licked, then sucked her nipple. She moaned, and it was all the encouragement he needed to keep up his ministrations though her efforts to remove her boots required more work from him to keep her upper body still so he could pleasure her.

Movement was a little jagged, but within minutes he had her naked and laid back on the bed. He pressed kisses over every part of her body, and allowed himself to touch her with both hands, to analyze how she felt with his cybernetic part compared to his human one. The experience was so different. With humanity it was merely flesh upon flesh, but with the cybernetic hand, there was an underlying knowledge. He could sense a change in her temperature, how such touches either heightened her arousal or lessened it.

"I'm going to have so much fun with you."

She gazed up at him with hooded eyes. "I want more than simple pleasure, Hemi. Make me fucking scream."

Her demand would be his ultimate goal and he focused on pleasuring her, from nipples to pussy. His mouth and fingers worked their magic. He found his stamina wasn't fatiguing as he tongued Sophia's clit — a quick trace and he found her soaking wet for him. Wasn't difficult to slide two fingers inside her, and this time his cybernetics were attuned to her every need. As she gripped him tight and started to grind against his movements, he responded in kind, working her into a frenzy.

Wasn't long before she screamed his name, her release coating him. He was more turned on than ever and not overheating. The miracle of it, he didn't feel dizzy or overwhelmed.

"I'm going to pound into you and erase all traces of any past lovers."

Freeing his cock from his pants, he angled himself over her, guiding toward her entrance. Then he leaned down and whispered into her ear. "I'm going to fuck you like no one has."

"Please," she begged. "I need it. Fill me up."

"Dirty mouth, Sophia…be careful what you wish for." Before he'd dreamed of being gentle, taking her slowly, but he was failing horribly at keeping that thought at the forefront. Not when she demanded something completely different. He slid into her with enough force to make her gasp.

She was tight, so very tight. Her delicious channel snugly embraced him like a driver inside a racer, providing a cocoon for his cock. He was lost to movement, sensation. How long had it been? No experience had provided anything to him like this before. She wasn't a still, lie back and enjoy herself type of lover either.

Sophia propped herself up on her elbows and rocked her hips, moving with him. As he pulled away, she drove back up, over and over, as if the mere seconds he was separated from her were far too long.

Every movement was another lesson in working toward a release that fast approached. He hadn't even taken himself in hand until the other day. Six months was a long time, but worth the wait, for his reward was her. Her skin was coated in a thin sheen of sweat. Her panting breaths matched his and something about the way she focused her gaze on their joining turned him on like no other.

"Faster. Please."

At her plea, he removed his hands from her hips, and wrapped her up in his arms, rocking back on his knees. He propped her up so her thighs were supported by his, and surged upward as she opposed his movements. She screamed and he kept going, driving forward to ensure he hit every bit of her. To let her feel every movement of his.

His cybernetic leg, in fact the entire half of his body that was no longer human, absorbed the heat and electrical connection as if feeding from it and seemed to enhance his strength. He felt rejuvenated, not tired in the least. Urging himself to go faster to the point that he was nearly lifting her off of him, he plunged her down onto his cock.

The wail she let out came amid curses and his name. Desperate for release, she grabbed onto his shoulders, digging her fingernails into him.

"I'm going to…I'm going to…fuck!"

Her release triggered his own. Unable to hold back, he wrenched her from him as he spilled seed.

"You could have kept going," she replied, crawling back toward him. "My parents ensured I had the same implant as those on the Uppers receive. I can only get pregnant if I so choose."

Birthrates were often low anyway, but he never took chances like that, refusing to leave bastards or orphans in his wake. "I still wouldn't risk you that way."

She reached for his half-hard cock. At a mere touch, it was already stiffening again. "Then let me clean you up before we go again."

"That needy for me now?"

Leaning down, while she kept her gaze on him, she licked him from root to tip, cleaning away the evidence of his release. "I told you, I don't want to stop until these sheets are wet."

"That's a promise I can keep."

Chapter Seventeen

Sophia rolled over to hear the morning bell toll. She'd overslept... *Shit!* Gaia had told her to be at the Watering Hole first thing. They had plans, except each night she found herself with plans of her own.

Hemi...she absently reached across the bed for him. Usually, they fell asleep with him spooning behind her, holding her tightly, but always somewhere in the wee early hours of the morning, he moved away, onto his back, spreading out as much as he could. As if his body ached to stretch.

Her hand brushed against the hair on his arm. She didn't mind his human side compared to the sleek, cool surface of his cybernetic components. She loved all of him. Rolling over, she dared to lift the sheet and examine him in his full glory.

Of course, he probably would disagree with her. The scarred, mottled, white and red flesh where the cybernetic component melded to his human pieces was the only remaining evidence of where he'd been burned from the racer fire.

But the scarring was from the neck down, across his torso, making him a half-human, half-cybernetic hybrid. Thankfully, his gorgeous cock had been spared…said cock was starting to get semi-hard. She was tempted to suck him off until he awoke.

They'd spent nearly every night of the last week fucking like crazy as soon as they left the Watering Hole, sometimes barely making it to the bedroom before engaging in sexual surrender. She was a sucker for everything he wanted to do. Depraved or not, they were trying all sorts of positions, and pushing his stamina to the absolute limit. He'd mentioned once or twice how she was helping him, even as she was unsure how copious amounts of sex could assist him in his recovery.

They still needed to talk about that part. The part where he explained more about his newfound abilities and how he'd gone from breaking out in a panic at simply kissing her to having the stamina of a racing engine supplied with endless amounts of sludge fuel.

"You're staring at me."

"Hmm, am I?" she asked as she let her gaze land on his face…those golden eyes and the dark tan of his skin, the black eyebrows. He was so painful to look at. So damn beautiful.

"You've got a weird expression on your face. What's wrong?"

How did she tell him that this last week had blown all her girlhood fantasies to oblivion and she dreaded whatever the future held? She didn't want to lose this. But that was some deep shit for another day.

"Just admiring your strength. You survived that crash, the fire and became this."

"A hideous being that only you can bear to look at?" The flirtatious look in his eyes was the sole indication he wasn't serious.

"Hush your mouth. I'm sure there are plenty of women wandering around Frog Lick that wish I would just disappear. Even with your alterations, they would still want you. So quit dismissing my compliments."

He rolled toward her, covering himself up once more with the sheet. "If you keep them coming, I'll stop. Now what else is on your mind?"

"You promised before you left me to rescue Jack, you'd tell me more about this." She touched his cybernetic shoulder. "The whole communicating without speaking. How you're suddenly all right after Jack's rescue when before you were hellbent on taking things slow."

Hemi glanced around the room, as if looking at her would unravel his very thoughts. She had no clue where his mind was at, but...

"You can trust me with this stuff, you know that, right? No matter what we did back when we were kids, I never told anyone. There are still some parts of our exploits that are unknown. Believe in me, please. I can be trusted with this information."

"Yeah, I know... It's not really all my secret to tell because the others are involved, too. But I'll share what I can." He held his hand out to her and she took it, letting him pull her in close to cuddle.

"I'm not detailed into the tech, but Gina found a way to manipulate the electronic impulse feeds that can allow us to communicate. We can send codes through our implants if we're within a certain radius, which works well when someone needs to get in touch with everyone fast and we may be in different parts of Frog Lick."

How marvelous that would be, to silently communicate with others. "Makes me a little envious. I'd have a way to talk to you without ever saying anything out loud."

"Don't wish such a thing on yourself. To get to this point involved a lot of pain, struggle and self-loathing. Also, a lot of anger."

"Tell me more."

"First, I'll say this. The reason why things are different is because Jack and Shannon went to Auster in search of something that could stop the natural degradation that was attributed to the original tech used for the cybernetics. I can't share more details except they found a solution and it's provided healing I dreamed impossible. Whatever they found has somehow magically made my two halves harmonious and given me feeling. I don't think it's the same for all of us, but for me... I'm not dismissing such a gift."

She lifted her head to stare at him, searching his face for any signs of discontent. "Is that why you're not angry anymore?"

"I'm still upset. There are things I regret and a few grudges I hold...nothing against you. Though, I won't lie, if people hadn't made the choices they had, I might not be lying here holding you close to me. The tradeoff was worth it."

She couldn't help the grin. "You're saying I'm worth any type of sacrifice?"

"No, I mean, we don't get to spend the day in bed. I have places to be, you told Gaia you would be there before the bell... We're already late."

She reached between his legs, but before she could grab a hold of him, he slid out from under the sheet and right off the bed while holding her safely in place. "You're really walking away right now?"

"I think it's for the best. Besides, we'll have tonight."

The words were of little comfort to her, because deep down, she was unsure how many more 'tonights' there would be. Seemed like any day her parents would arrive and invade her idyllic existence.

"You're right, of course. I'll settle for tonight, but it will be your turn. I get to have my way with you."

"Your wish is my command."

If only that were true.

* * * *

Hemi was in a damn good mood as he walked into the mechanics bay.

"You're late."

"Yeah, well…it's not like you haven't been late a time or two because of a beautiful woman, Jack."

Jack had recovered quickly after they had rescued him from Bridget's clutches, though he was still missing two fingers. While they kept moving toward the end result of getting the racer primed for Hemi and the championship race coming up in two months, there was the undercurrent of tension and vigilance.

No one knew when Bridget might attempt to strike. Additionally, the note that had brought the fingers and Shannon's additional confessions told everyone that Bridget had spies within Frog Lick.

How? No one was sure. It was a task Drag was working with Rune on. Rune and Petal, along with a few others, were covertly watching those in town and trying to determine who wasn't supporting them.

Add in Gina's urge to randomly run tests on Hemi and the others to make sure the nanites were working properly and the only thing keeping a smile on Hemi's face was the sexual gratification and memories he was making with Sophia.

"Don't let him fool you," Gina called out. "He was late this morning too."

Hemi eyed Jack with speculation.

"Shannon's needy."

"Or you can't keep your dick in your pants, either works."

Jack chuckled. "You're one to talk."

"Exactly what we were doing this morning, conversating." Hemi got farther into the bay and noticed the back doors were pulled up. "What's the plan today?"

"Taking the racer out. You're driving, and Jack is shotgun. Want to see how you do." Gina popped up the hood as she spoke and started to check fluid levels. "It's about time you got back behind a wheel. Doesn't have to be any fancy speeds or heading to the racing dome today. Just sit in the driver's seat a minute, fire the engine up and drive it up down the main strip a couple times."

"Simple enough, right?" Jack asked.

Hemi was sure his friend didn't miss how he'd frozen feet from the car and was having trouble willing himself to move closer. "Yeah, easy."

The problem was he'd ridden in haulers since the accident, but he'd yet to actually wrap his hands around a wheel. Even now, sweat beads gathered on his forehead.

"Hey."

Hemi had missed Jack coming up, standing shoulder to shoulder with him. "I'll be with you and we don't have to rush things. Got all day."

Hemi nodded in response, vaguely aware of the words since his pulse was pounding in his ears. He forced himself to take one, then two, followed by three steps forward. Slow, steady progress to get to the racer itself. He braced both hands on the door, one at the top of the frame and another on the handle.

If I'm not a racer, what am I?

The question he'd been asking himself for the last seven months was now in front of him. He had to face this fear, right? Needed to find a way to climb into the driver's seat and fire up the racer. To feel the engine rumble to life.

He opened the door, then stood immobile again.

"Doing great, Hemi."

Yep, so damn good he had no sense of movement or time. Jack was already on the other side of the vehicle and climbing in.

"Take your time."

Time was something he didn't have, though. This would prove if he could or if he couldn't. If not, then he needed to be done here in Full Throttle. Move on to find the next path for his future. There were plenty of mechanics here, and compared with Gina the genius AI, Hemi could be lumped into the idiot category.

Fuck it.

He climbed into the seat and shut the door. The air around him grew thick, like trying to breathe in a smoky room. His chest was heavy, vision blurry and no matter what he did, his arms were like processing sludge, viscous and slippery. He couldn't touch the wheel even though he knew that was what he was supposed to do.

The memories assailed him...the roars from the crowd as he passed the finish line, the pressure of his leg and foot on the accelerator easing up as he started his victory lap then coming into the turn. The beep, the click of something releasing then fire everywhere, burning his whole body.

What if he touched the starter and it triggered something all over again? Hemi's hands were up, palms facing out from his chest, and he couldn't do anything.

"A couple deep breaths, Hemi. This car has been checked four times for anything strange. There is no bomb, no mishap. So much maintenance you would think the racer was Snapper's child."

It was. Hemi tried to grab onto Jack's words like a rope he could climb to freedom. The reminders were helpful but still not enough.

"I burned alive in the racer. Half of my body ignited immediately like I was a perfect conductor for the source. I hear what you're saying, but my brain can't... I can't risk my life turning this thing on."

There might have been a thread of embarrassment deep beneath the fear and panic in his tone, but his mental state was such that he didn't care. They could call him weak and any other number of names and he'd probably shrug them off. What mattered was this moment of truth and he couldn't face this. The irrational thoughts reigned supreme.

He was dripping sweat now and still frozen.

"Fine, it's all good. Care if I swap seats with you then?"

Hemi opened the car door and slid out fast, as if the racer were already burning. When Jack got in the driver's seat, he glanced up at Hemi.

"You can hop in with me? Play passenger."

Hemi shook his head as he paced back and forth the length of the vehicle. "No, I don't think that's a good idea. Run Gina's tests for me, please, and I'll talk to Drag. Looks like Full Throttle needs a new lead driver."

Forcing himself to say the words out loud lifted a bit of the weight on his chest. This uncertainty he'd been carrying for months now had been confirmed. He despised himself for feeling relief, but outside the racer, he could breathe again.

"Fine. I'll do it. But don't think we're done talking about this. You'll always be our lead driver." Jack started up the racer then drove it out of the bay and behind the building. Hemi could admire the craftsmanship, the clean purr of the engine as it roared and even the sleek lines of the body. The damn thing was a piece of art. No matter what Jack said, Hemi had no business driving the masterpiece.

The main entrance door opened and slammed shut behind him. Running feet scrambled and slapped against the floor, paired with the shouting. "Hemi! Hemi!"

A younger boy, one who worked for Gaia at the Watering Hole, came to a halt right in front them. "Hemi, Drag needs you across the street right now."

"What's wrong?" The day wasn't shaping up to be as idyllic as Hemi had hoped. The happiness of his morning had already been dampened.

"Sophia's parents have arrived."

Chapter Eighteen

Sophia was spread out in one of the booths, books and scraps of paper with additional information before her. She scribbled in her journal, a bound book of pressed paper scrap that Gaia and Petal had presented her with after her first meeting of the Frog Lick Social Club.

"This is your book to carve out the future you want."

Funny word, carve, because she was writing instead. Fertilizing soil techniques, planting recommendations, methods to keep away pests and safeguard crops and the mechanics behind aqueducts and hydroponic filtering. Of all of this was what Full Throttle had really been working on behind the scenes.

They were on their way to being self-sufficient without the need for ship-building and racing wins, though they didn't have enough materials yet and they needed more supplies to support growth.

Keeping food growing is no easy job.

And judging by the number of pages she'd filled already, this would be a challenge. The mornings were spent studying, note-taking. After lunch, she served time in the trenches with the other woman and volunteers who worked the airponics gardens, along with the soil-based gardens they were starting to propagate. She'd never thought herself much of a student or with the ability to make things grow, but the prospect of her efforts feeding those who went hungry in Aurestral sustained her.

This was the future she wanted, one where she earned her people's freedom from selling themselves and suffering.

Teija slid into the booth seat across from her.

"Good things never do last," she murmured as she kept jotting down her notes.

"You knew I'd be back sooner or later…turns out it's later than I would have preferred and sooner than you would like." Teija spoke quietly. She didn't bother to look at him. His bangles rattled as he moved his arms.

"Where did you go first? Because I'm sure if you'd gone to my parents, the sooner would have occurred."

He didn't respond and that was when she put her writing tool down. Taking him in, she noticed his gaze wasn't as bright, his frame tense and lips dry. There was a bruise on his upper-right cheek, fading but still mottled with purple, blue and yellow. He'd opted for full coverings across his arms and chest, rather than the short-sleeved vests or tunics he preferred.

"Did they hurt you?" She genuinely hated the idea he'd been punished because of her choices, reminding her too much of how Hemi had suffered for her as well. *No more of that.*

"I asked them for five minutes before they enter. We're down to two. Let me say I tried to convince your fiancé otherwise. I thought…well, I believed foolish things, which I'll tell you about in detail another time. He wouldn't back down, so I was sent back to Aurestral with an armed escort and delivered the news of your defection to your parents.

"They are here. They expect your agreement to return. The marriage contract will still be honored, if you renounce —"

"This farce." Her father's voice was sharp as he pounded a fist against the table. "You've shamed us. Now more than ever. This embarrassment can't stand, Sophia Regalia Archer. We have never asked much, but this is the one thing we can't go back on."

Out of time indeed. Sophia dared to glance her father's direction. Her eyes were the same as his and it was like looking into a grayish-blue storm staring back at her. She could return the favor.

"If I don't want to go, I won't." It was the simplest answer she could give because she was tired of being backed into a corner.

"We'll lose everything."

"There's another way." She saw Drag approach with slow measured steps. Her father's bodyguards were already there, swords drawn. The twin pair of men would attack only if her father was threatened, or by his command.

"I seek an audience with you, Aurestral leader." Drag's confidence never wavered even with swords at his throat.

"Who are you? You are not the one who married my daughter."

Drag shook his head. "No, I am the Full Throttle leader and I'm somewhat aware of problems plaguing your town and people. I'd like to explain how we might mutually benefit each other."

"What do you want in return?"

"Ally consideration and agreement my gang won't be attacked or threatened due to whatever transpired during Sophia's visit here."

Her father frowned then his shoulders slumped. Sophia had always viewed him as a larger-than-life force, stronger than even the drug cartel leaders of Earth. One who had a plan, a vision, and was always ready to counteract anything thrown his direction. But here she saw someone worn and ravaged by life, near defeated.

"Ravi and Louis, put your weapons away. Full Throttle leader, lead me somewhere we might talk privately. Felucia, Daughter, Teija, you will attend as well." Her father had spoken softly, but still commanding. He'd tolerate no objection to his decree and Sophia didn't have any if it meant her father would consider Drag's offer.

This was her chance to show something of herself. They didn't need her overzealous fiancé. Not once this alliance proposal was made. It would be the start of something brand new.

Drag nodded and pointed to a small hallway that was off to the left of the main stage area. Sophia was familiar with the area, as Gaia had pointed out it was a secure and quiet space where Full Throttle leaders met. While Drag was their official voice, she was well aware there were many others who had input into how things operated in this gang.

She slid out of her seat, and noticed Gaia already standing off to the side.

"I'll gather your things. You don't have to worry about them. Collect them from the bar when you're finished."

Sophia smiled at the other woman. "You're too kind. Thank you."

Teija fell into step beside her as she followed her father, his guards, her mother and Drag. Her mother didn't spare a single glance for her. The older woman never did care for confrontations and usually ignored Sophia unless instructing her on how to behave.

"I'm sorry." Teija's head was lowered, and he was watching his feet as they walked.

"For what?"

"Leaving you, thinking I had to take some sort of action."

Sophia shrugged. "It's okay. You did what was best, what you believed in."

"I love him, Sophia." His gaze flew to hers and there she saw anguish and heartbreak.

"Who?"

The answer concerned her. Teija had always kept very tight-lipped about his emotions. He didn't share feelings for the sake of the boundaries between them, even when Sophia often confessed everything because Teija was her only friend.

"Caden."

She couldn't help the laugh that bubbled up and out of her lips, a little thing that became a chortle. She covered her mouth. Her mother sharply turned to shush at her and that didn't help at all.

"She'll be fine, ma'am," Teija responded and took a hold of Sophia by the shoulders. "What's so damn funny?"

"Us, the pair of us, getting all roped up in attachments. Ones that don't benefit us at all. I take it he wasn't going to give up his shot at having his own gang for you?"

Teija let go of her abruptly and she stumbled a couple steps. "Easy guess. Not very smart of me to take a risk. I was dumb like you but thought maybe if you were brave enough to try, then I could be too."

"Brave—"

"Where is she?" Hemi's booming voice and the slam of the Watering Hole door brought everyone to a stop.

Conversation and the sound of utensils in use ceased. Her father's guards immediately drew weapons and moved to the back of the group behind Teija and Sophia. They'd almost entered the hallway where she turned to face Hemi, whose entire frame was outlined by the brightness from the sun, the front of him cast in shadow. The door closed as Hemi began to march swiftly toward them. The guards were still ready to attack.

Someone would have to interfere, but in the moment, Sophia was too in awe of the way Hemi had come. A message had somehow been delivered to him and instead of running away, here he was.

"Looks like where my risk was for nothing, yours may have worked," Teija whispered to her.

I can only hope.

Hemi recognized the guards. The pair always flanked the Aurestral leader, Papal, duty bound to protect him with their life. It confirmed that their marriage was on its last legs. Papal and his wife would take back Sophia at all costs, of that Hemi was sure. Especially if they knew Sophia had married him.

Do they know?

"Better put those swords away before I break them." He couldn't help the challenge. Adrenaline rushed through him on the heels of his overwhelming fear about being in that damn racer. He channeled the rush into anger and concern for Sophia.

If there was one thing he was good at, it was sacrificing his own comfort for her. No matter how hard he'd tried to stop being that way, it had been ingrained within him from the moment they met. He'd always save her, always shield her.

"Hemi?" Papal called his name like a question.

He looked toward the older man, the one who'd ensured he had to leave Aurestral, face potential sale into the clubs or death. Papal hadn't wanted him around to tempt his daughter anymore. He'd sworn to never give Hemi a chance to marry her.

"This! This is why you came here, for him?" The outrage and how the anger there turned the older gray-haired man's face red made Hemi outrageously happy.

Hemi smiled. "Upset she still chose me?"

"Kill this man. Kill him now."

The words were to be expected. He knew how much the older man hated him for his invisible tug on his daughter. This wasn't the first time he'd been threatened. Hemi squared off, ready to fight.

Time to see what this body is made of.

Instead, Sophia was all of a sudden in front of him. She plastered her back against him, spreading her arms wide. Her bodyguard Teija flanked them both and squarely dispelled any sword swipes that Papal's trained killers attempted.

"Enough!" Drag's voice echoed through the room and seemed to bring everyone to halt. "You said, Aurestral leader, you would listen and consider."

"Before I knew this bastard was here. He's the one, isn't he?" Papal pointed at Sophia. "You married him, didn't you?"

She flipped her arms and wrapped them partially around Hemi's body. "I did, and I would again."

A part of his heart soared in admiration for how she didn't try to hide what they shared, their connection. How she'd dived in front of him to protect him, bringing Teija along with her. Teija, who she'd always roped into her schemes time and again. He'd disliked Hemi, but only because he feared the repercussions he'd suffer by the association.

"Aurestral leader, I say again…consideration must be given to what I propose. If you do not agree after, you can discuss next steps, but blood will not be spilled in this common area. We no longer work like that within Frog Lick and I won't have you damage years of repair due to a prejudice for one man." Drag shocked Hemi. His diplomatic words were a surprise because Hemi had never seen their leader involved in conversations with other gangs. The words they had for Bridget were less than accommodating, but here Drag artfully wove a convincing, respectful story.

"Fine, fine…but he comes as well. I want him present when the judgment is delivered. I won't let him run again only to be a thorn in my side many more years from now."

The group proceeded to move forward, guards sheathing their weapons and taking up positions around Papal and now Sophia's mother, Felucia, who'd moved closer to him.

"Guess we should follow them?" Hemi encircled Sophia's waist and gave her a gentle squeeze.

Shannon turned and faced him, before wrapping him in a hug and pecking a kiss to his cheek. "When did you know?"

"Drag sent a messenger."

"And you came?" The surprise on her face stunned him.

"Why, did you think I wouldn't?"

Taking a step back, she linked their hands and gently tugged. "Because it's not your battle and you have your own issues to face."

"You knew they were going to try and put me in that racer today." The change of subject distracted from the now, but part of him hated being so vulnerable here. Sure, he'd called her out for the same thing, but in that way they were alike. "That's not as important as this, in case you need me."

"Maybe you should both focus on whatever comes next, because if Papal doesn't agree, he's going to demand Hemi's head," Teija said from behind them as they worked to catch up with the group already filing into the back room.

Those were sobering thoughts. "Drag won't let that happen. But I can't say he'll be able to make you stay."

"Then you can come with me. We can fix Aurestral together." Sophia's smile was bright, as if her response held the easiest solution.

Can I go back? Do I want to? There had been plenty of reasons to leave there, and there were plenty to depart now. His future was uncertain. He needed to solve his problems, not be burdened with the future of others.

Hemi kept silent, not responding to Sophia's statement. Everything inside him wanted to separate from her and run like hell. It was hard enough to be responsible for one person...a few thousand would be impossible.

They entered the room where the others were already seated, the Aurestral party on one side of the room, with Full Throttle on the other. Sophia chose to sit next to Hemi. He sat next to Drag and of course, Teija stayed on their side too, which evened the numbers.

"Well, your name, Full Throttle leader?"

"Drag, and yours?"

Hemi spoke first. "It's Papal. His wife is Felucia."

He had no smiles for them, and they had none in return—only cold and defiant eyes, displeasure at his connection now to their family when Papal had sworn there would be none.

"Yes, now, Hemi, I want proof. Prove you married my damn daughter."

Hemi glanced at Sophia and she gave an agreeing nod. At the same time, they pulled up their sleeves to reveal the inked tattoo of Full Throttle's mark, along with their initials inked within.

If asked, Hemi would have proudly said that part of his reasoning for the marriage was just to see the look on Papal's face when he found out. Though nothing compared to the clenched fists that Papal pounded against the top of this thighs then the primal scream that started as a deep low bellow.

When the man finally finished, all traces of his true feelings were locked away, controlled and measured. "Your alliance proposal should be swift, for my animosity spreads like an inferno."

Drag cleared his throat. "It's come to my attention that your people struggle with adequate food supplies, whereas my town has developed the means to reduce food shortage and provide alternatives for all our members. In exchange for your willingness to compensate us for Marsanium-refined ore, we would be willing to share these methods with you. My team has even begun to familiarize your daughter with such information so she could help with growing these skills among your people."

The offer was met with silence. No doubt Papal would dismiss the solution. The man was too good at holding a grudge to actually care about anyone beside himself. That was the problem. When Sophia had told Drag and most likely others of how those in Aurestral suffered, of the orphans and adults who sold themselves like possessions for bed, food and water...she had left out the part where her parents, their leaders, didn't care and looked the other way because profits and success lined their pockets. In return for the lack of a recent win or the declining output the Aurestral mines produced, their slave trade was lucrative. They had direct contact with the pleasure moon, Callisto.

Sophia probably had no clue, not when her focus wasn't on her parents and on the people around her. She was searching for a bandage instead of severing the festering wound from the body. Nothing could heal this unless entirely new leadership took over.

"I believe you are misunderstood in all the facets of our operation, but an agreement for processed ore might be reached. We have seen a decline in our outputs."

Because you've sold off any decent labor and use children.

"Trading with you would help our ship production, but what happens when you regain your contract?"

"That may not be for some time. The commission denied our appeal, so the original sentence still stands, and we're only two years in."

"Have you considered re-locating some of these hungry mouths elsewhere? They might find more success in another gang, even in Aurestral."

Hemi did his best to keep his expression neutral, but the offer Papal made was disgusting. The bastard was aiming for more bodies to trade, bodies to auction off. Because what did they sell when they had no flash? Themselves.

"No, afraid that's not on the table. I promised them a life here, in Frog Lick. If they choose to leave on their own, that's one thing, but as their leader, I speak for their wishes. Not the other way around. They've elected me to represent their interests."

Papal chuckled. "Elected? Like some sort of fake Upper Parliament thing? You know Mars is still fighting for a voice in a universe that doesn't care about us. Sticking to the old ways, right to rule by power and appointment, is far better than lowly people speaking. Half of them don't know what they want."

Even Hemi saw the tension in Drag's frame. Papal did try a person's patience far more than a normal person.

"Yes, well again. You operate Aurestral as you like, and we'll take care of Full Throttle. Are we in agreement?"

Papal considered the words with a look at his wife. Felucia only blinked a couple times, almost imperceptible to anyone else, but the woman had made it an art to communicate with her husband without words. While he'd never openly say he valued her opinion, he did take it into consideration.

"Fine, we are aligned. You can draft a contract and I'll sign it, but only under one additional condition. Sophia is to go back with us."

Hemi knew this was coming. It wasn't a surprise they wanted her back. She was as much of a bargaining chip as any other human being that lived in Aurestral, meant for them to sell or trade however they deemed fit. At least, he believed that was how they saw her.

"Not unless you let Hemi come with me." Sophia's declaration only made Hemi regret everything even more because no one was getting what they wanted out of this, except maybe Papal himself.

"Sophia..." He reached for her hand and held it between both of his. For a split second he just enjoyed the fact he could feel her with his cybernetic one. *Still a miracle.* "We knew this is what it would come to."

"Are you willing to give us up?"

"I don't want to go back." Those were the truest words he'd ever spoken. Twice today he'd let his feelings emerge and twice he was ready for the backlash. Though, instead of the slap on the cheek he expected, Sophia shrugged off his touch.

"Honesty is always best, even when it hurts." She faced her parents. "I'm still not okay with this, holding a good deal hostage for having me back. We need to talk."

"Full Throttle, would you mind if we had the room to discuss things further while you draft the contract?"

"We will return once it's ready." Drag touched Hemi's shoulder gently.

A glance and Hemi followed Drag out of the room. Blood roared in his ears, and he was like an emotionless blob as he walked toward the bar.

"Hemi, let's convene at the mechanics bay. We'll need the others."

Then the door to the Watering Hole slammed open for the second time that day, but instead of Hemi being the one responsible, it was another man he didn't recognize with long blonde hair, flanked by a woman with burning red locks and a shifty-looking person with glowing eyes, covered head to toe in fabric.

"Where is she?"

Chapter Nineteen

"I refuse to return if you're going to force me to marry. I'm already married."

Sophia's father chuckled. "Really, you are? Your would-be husband made it clear already he doesn't intend to return to Aurestral. Caden would take you however you are."

Yeah, because he doesn't want me.

But she couldn't say that because the truth didn't matter to her father. He had a deal in place, and he'd do whatever he could to ensure it was completed.

Teija was still present and he stepped up beside her. "Maybe this is for the best."

"You too? Why is everyone against what I have with Hemi?"

Her mother sighed. "Because he's obviously not the right fit. You are bound to Aurestral, the way your father and I are. We owe the people our best and with Hemi you won't find it."

"We? Does this mean you're considering what I said about not handing over the run of Aurestral to Caden?" She hated the flare of hope in her heart. No matter what they said, she still didn't want to leave Hemi behind. She desired both, Hemi and to help her people. Why was it so difficult to make both happen?

She'd focus on wearing them down about the marriage to Caden, then worry about Hemi afterwards. Except luck wasn't on her side as the door to the room burst open and Drag walked in with the very man she'd been discussing.

"I don't understand why you won't let Bridget back here to speak with the Aurestral leader. I've offered her the chance at an audience."

Drag let out a low growl. "Full Throttle and Macintosh are currently at odds and she won't be permitted into this inner area. If you want to negotiate terms, then depart with your group and do so in her gang-town. I would suggest the decision be made sooner."

"Caden." Her father's greeting was far more jovial than Sophia cared for. "You came."

"As soon as I received your message." He didn't head to her parents' side, though. Instead he stopped right in front of her. "Is it true? Did you decide to marry another?"

He played the part of concerned fiancé well, though Sophia didn't miss Teija's yearning look in the man's direction. As far as she was concerned, he'd hurt her best friend and for such a transgression, she'd never trust whatever came out of his mouth.

"I did. I'm afraid my heart was engaged elsewhere."

Caden turned, taking in the room's occupants. "Then where is he?"

"He stepped out."

Her father took this as his moment to put more of a shadow on the situation. "I'm afraid he stepped back completely. He has no interest in Aurestral."

Caden shook his head, the sympathy in his features the kind of acting she'd rarely seen before. "That's devastating to hear. Sophia, if you wish, I'll let this marriage stand if you agree to come back to Aurestral where we can find some way to rule jointly, side-by-side. I understand a heart's desire." He glanced at Teija, whose gaze softened a bit, filling with hope.

Seems we're both suckers for a pretty face.

"What are you proposing?"

"That you hear me out, hear Macintosh out. They seek an alliance. One that might prove very lucrative."

Sophia would disagree. Bridget...the woman not let in, was responsible for Hemi's accident, if Drag and all of them in Full Throttle were to be believed. She'd also kidnapped one of their members and hurt several of them. Snippets of the tales had been coming to her ever since Hemi returned. The woman and her gang couldn't be trusted.

"That's not possible for me." She'd stand her ground no matter what and there were certain things she refused to budge on. "I've recently discussed an alliance with the Full Throttle leader, Drag. I want to continue that opportunity. If you agree to dismiss Macintosh, and are open to me continuing my marriage, I will return to Aurestral with you and we can amicably discuss how to move forward."

Drag appeared impressed with her negotiating. Though her parents weren't.

"It's not open for debate—"

"I agree with your suggested plan of action and I'd love to hear more about this proposed alliance," Caden replied, cutting her father off.

Papal Archer was redder than Mars dust. He tugged at the collar of his shirt. "Don't you think we should discuss this amongst ourselves first, Caden?"

She wasn't sure how she felt about her father being hamstrung by his would-be successor, though Caden appeared to be far better at negotiations than she'd expected.

"You never said he was so charismatic," she whispered to Teija.

"Would you expect anything less from someone who tempted me?"

Valid point.

Conversation continued between Caden and her parents. She was only catching half of the snippets. Something about for them not to worry, to let him take care of things. That this was what they'd wanted, right? Retirement, less stress.

Concerning to say the least, but she wouldn't affect things by staying here. Her parents were in thrall and to keep them off her back, she needed to negotiate things with this potential business partner, because he wouldn't be her husband.

No, she refused to replace Hemi with a pale, blonde complete opposite. The man barely had muscles and while he had a kind manner of speaking and a nice tone, he wasn't what she desired in the least. Sophia found it ironic that Teija found Caden attractive.

"Then we leave before dusk." Caden's words were a proclamation rather than a question.

She couldn't depart that fast. "How about first thing in the morning? I need to gather my things, speak with my husband."

Because no way would the last words they shared be his truth bomb about not wanting to return to Aurestral. She needed to talk more, to understand what type of future they had. Of course, foolishly she'd believed they had more time. If she'd known her family and her ex-fiancé were descending upon Frog Lick today, she would've forced Hemi to stay in bed longer this morning.

So many wishes, but I need a little more time.

"If that's what's needed." Caden pointed to Drag. "Full Throttle leader, do you have accommodations for us?"

"We have a few outbuildings...I mean homes, that haven't been occupied yet. They should serve the purpose you need. Food and drink can be retrieved here."

"And the cost?"

Drag shook his head. "No cost. We offer this to you freely as passers through."

Her mother looked surprised, as did Caden for a brief second. Her father seemed preoccupied with his own thoughts. No doubt around how he'd completely lost all hope of being the one in charge of the next steps.

"That's very generous of you."

"It's how things work in Frog Lick. Rest assured, we believe in making allies of almost anyone, or at the least being hospitable."

Sophia elbowed Teija and motioned toward the door. Her bodyguard responded with a firm shake of the head, but that was the problem, this mess.

Whatever the future held, she needed to get out of here to get as much time with Hemi as possible.

Drag continued. "If you'll connect with my brother, Rune, he is waiting at the bar in the main area. He can direct you to where you'll stay. Looks a lot like me, just no cybernetic arm. I need to see to some unwanted guests."

With that statement made, Drag headed for the door, as both her parents and Caden started to gather together again. She snuck in right behind him and out the door.

"Is it true Bridget is here?"

Drag slammed his cybernetic fist through the wall beside them. The outburst of violence was answer enough, though Sophia wasn't sure why Bridget elicited such a reaction from him.

"She won't be for long." The words were laced with a deep thread of anger. There was a story here, but Sophia didn't have the courage to ask or the time to spare.

"Is Hemi still here?"

"I don't know. He was at the bar when your fiancé and Bridget arrived."

She pushed past Drag and jogged into the main room, scanning for Hemi's face. The patrons present were few and she only recognized Rune and Petal, stationed at the bar like Drag had said. Gaia was wiping down the bar.

Sophia headed toward her first. Trusting the woman to know more than anyone else. "Gaia, where did Hemi go?"

"Not one hundred percent sure, but he looked a bit sad when he departed, said he needed to clear his head.

If he's not at home, you might check the mechanics bay or the shipping bay."

"Thanks." She spared another look at the others and found Drag already marching out the door. No doubt to take care of unwanted guests. She needed to find Hemi, to talk to him... *Convince him to come with me.*

Because she didn't want to go alone, and she'd need an ally for whatever Caden had planned. Something about the man spoke of mistrust and hidden agendas. Even though Teija seemed fooled, she refused to be.

Things were in motion she couldn't stop, but damn if she was going to give up the one good part of her life.

* * * *

"How much longer will this take?" Bridget asked. Her voice echoed off the cavernous space that was the shipping bay. More like a graveyard, since the ships were in so many various states of development.

The tip of her shapely leather boot tapped against the floor with a steady beat, showcasing her impatience, while her assassin bodyguard, the Innkucai, slowly paced back and forth. That tall, scary androgynous being freaked Hemi a bit. There was no reading of their physical features—the Innkucai was swathed head to toe in material, not necessarily clothing, with an overall covering and a hood over their head.

They didn't speak, just watched and paced. Their glowing eyes put Hemi in the mind of something that could see right through him. He shivered.

"I asked you a question."

Hemi glanced at Bridget, whose arms were crossed over her chest. Her red hair acted as a beacon. Only then did a person take in the rest of her. Those green eyes, high cheekbones, angular but petite nose and the arrogant tilt of her lips implied she knew exactly what her beauty was capable of. This woman was weaponized.

"Whenever Drag gets here. That's how long." He'd wanted to leave, go home, find Jack, do anything besides stick around to see the fiancé's reunion with Sophia. No doubt Papal was excited at the Osprerine heir's appearance. Sophia would object, of course she'd complain, but eventually she'd come to see this was her path.

"You're the one who drove for Full Throttle in the last regional, right?"

Fuck Drag for appointing me as the one to watch this bitch.

"Yeah, what about it?"

"Well, congratulations are in order since you won. Though I'm shocked to see you still standing." Her smile was something only a devil would wear.

No way would he let her dig into his head. "Yes, I survived even with all your efforts to ensure I didn't."

"Did you though? I hear you're not quite human anymore. Rumor has it you can't even get in a racer." She clicked her tongue against her teeth. "That's just sad. A driver unable to race is, well…pathetic."

Hemi would show her pathetic. Fists locked, he started to approach her. He'd never believed in hitting a woman until now.

"Stop." Drag's voice called out. "Violence is what she wants. It's the only way to justify her actions, and we can't risk the possible allies."

Bridget's smile disappeared and Hemi stopped moving. The woman was truly a master manipulator with a goal to disrupt and destroy everything she encountered. Drag was standing beside him in seconds.

Hemi dared to glance at the man and was surprised to see Drag's face void of all emotion.

"It's good to see you, Drag. Though I expected more of the famed Full Throttle hospitality. I'm a bit disappointed."

"Can't say the same. Why the hell are you here?"

She sat up straight and uncrossed her arms, spreading her legs so she could rest her palms against the seat of the chair.

Hemi registered only a slight change in Drag's demeanor as the man ground his teeth together. Their past had settled in the air like a thick fog, blotting out any type of chance this might end amicably. Hemi had half-hoped they could talk their way out of a war.

"What can I say? I was just escorting a lost Osprerine searching for his beloved. He stumbled into Macintosh seeking her, but I'm afraid we didn't know much. Then I happened to hear you recently had some new folks in town. Didn't want a war to get started letting the Osprerine wander through Wespero territory. Seemed my duty to make sure he got here safely."

There might have been a single line of truth there, but most was bullshit. She hadn't needed to come herself. There were plenty of Macintosh drivers or errand runners to deliver that idiot here. He was about to say as much, when Drag beat him to the punch.

"But why you and your assassin companion? One would think you were going to attempt to murder me."

Damn. Drag didn't hesitate to call her out. Hemi found himself impressed by the directness.

"Aww, that would risk open warfare and it'd be hard for me to make it out of here alive. I'm just here to see if we can resolve our issues before things truly get out of hand." She stood up and approached Drag. "Would you believe me if I said I didn't really want a war? There's too much to risk."

Hemi watched as the Innkucai, the damn killer, stopped pacing and was at an angle that Hemi couldn't quite get a good look at. If they did launch an attack, Hemi and Drag wouldn't be ready.

"No, I don't believe you," Drag said. "If that was the case, then you would've left our racer alone. You wouldn't have kidnapped Jack. You wanted this conflict. You're going to reap the full impact. So, no lies. How worried are you about the information we stole?"

Bridget's eyes flashed in anger, and she held up her hand. The Innkucai stood down and resumed their pacing. *There was a threat.*

"You did steal something. Care to share what it is you think you know?"

Drag shook his head. "You'll just have to wait and see. But I promise whatever information we have will be shared when you least expect it. Now, why don't you leave and head on back to where you came from?"

"Damn you!" Bridget stomped her foot against the ground, her angry outburst echoing around them. "You could have just stayed, you know that, right?"

"And lose my humanity along with my arm? We're past the point of regrets, Bridget."

There was something different in her gaze, a longing that Hemi was shocked by. The dark details of what had occurred between these two had all the markings of a connection similar to what Hemi shared with Sophia. The big difference was Sophia wasn't a killer, and Bridget never seemed to hesitate at the opportunity to draw blood.

But as fast as she'd let the emotion leak out, she took a step back and the ice queen returned. "Well, we'll see about that. Seems I haven't made a good enough effort. I can promise to remedy that problem right away." She pivoted a slight bit toward the Innkucai. "We're going."

Walking around Drag, she stopped right beside him and leaned up, whispering something in his ear. Whatever it was, Hemi didn't catch it, but as she left, Drag picked up the metal chair and broke the thing in half. The two pieces clattered against the ground.

The ringing sound of the fall mixed with Bridget's laughter.

"That was creepy...you okay?" Hemi wouldn't dare to ask more. If Drag shared, then fine. If not, well...Hemi planned to leave anyway.

"Fine. Better than fine with her gone. The real question is, how are you?"

Hemi chuckled. "Really? I mean, I'm good."

"Good? You're going to let Sophia leave?"

"If that's what she wants." Because he wouldn't stand in the way of someone pursuing their dreams. A friend supported their friends.

"Maybe I had the wrong impression after all that chasing those Skeiron idiots and you and her with the closeness."

Hemi sighed and dragged a hand over his chin. "Yes, but caring for someone and abandoning who you are for them are two different things. Sophia and I have never hidden that from each other. We're friends, I helped her through a moment and she helped me. Now we go our separate ways—"

"She's still planning on staying married to you."

The words hit him square in the chest, tingling launched all over his cybernetic half. "When did she say that?"

"When I brought that fake-ass fiancé back to the room. She has no intention of severing the bond." Drag's way of staring him down bothered Hemi. *As if he has any room to judge anyone.*

"Well, I have to talk to her because —"

"You're not staying here either."

"How the hell did you know?"

"You're angry at us for saving you. You can't climb inside a racer without freezing up... Yes, I ran into Jack on my way here. That's why I was delayed. Maybe you thought we were unaware of your feelings, but I haven't missed your frustration or hesitance to talk to me, to anyone. Your work until now has been half-hearted as if you never lived in the first place. It's changed a bit since the second-gen injection." Drag stopped speaking and looked to Hemi to fill the gaps.

Why do I feel guilty? It spread, like sludge through the fuel injectors, coating him with embarrassment and shame. *No, don't fall there. You have a right to your feelings.*

"I didn't ask to be saved. To be turned into this." Hemi motioned to the left side of his body. "Sure, the injection made things fine, but it didn't change what's locked up in my head."

He tapped on his forehead a couple times. "I can't let it go. The nightmares aren't as bad, but they still exist. Every time I step in the bay, I'm angry all over again. Then driving...well, if Jack told you, then you know I can't get behind a wheel. If I'm not pulling my weight, doing what you brought me here to, then there is no point in staying."

"You can still stay. You're still Full Throttle." Drag closed their distance and clapped a hand on his shoulder. "Driving isn't the only thing we ask of you. Besides you're a brother to us, part of us."

Hemi shrugged Drag off. "No, I'm not. Never was. I came for the opportunity to drive. Signed on to bring Full Throttle a championship and prove my ability. You and your brothers are all leading members of this gang. Involved in aspects I'm not. I served a purpose, and I can't even fulfill that now."

"You can find a new path."

"I don't know what that is, and I need to leave here to discover it. Explore."

The silence was deafening, and Hemi couldn't bear to look Drag's way. Though he wasn't surprised when the Full Throttle leader found a way to sting a little deeper. "You sure this isn't just a reaction similar to when you left Aurestral? You feel like in order to re-invent yourself you have to run, but that's just it... You don't."

"I don't appreciate the psychoanalysis, but I do appreciate your kindness. Drag, this isn't where I need to be right now. I'm not sure where that's at, but as a friend, could you support me?"

Drag was the one to sigh now. He looked heavenward. "It's a tough ask, but I'll do my best. Don't be surprised if the others disagree as well. Whether you see it or not, you've become family. It's not about blood—it's about actions. You've proved over and over again what it means to be Full Throttle. Even holding to those ideals to help Sophia and Shannon."

Hemi blinked a couple times, willing away tears because no way would he cry, even as Drag's statement permeated to his very marrow and infected him with something he hadn't experienced before. They cared about him. It was why they'd saved him.

"Well, maybe outside of here, I can help others."

"Regardless, know you'll always have a place here." Drag held out his cybernetic hand, and Hemi grabbed on with his, giving a firm shake.

"Better get moving then," Hemi said as he turned toward the shipping bay entrance.

"Yeah…though you should know Sophia is looking for you. If you think I fought you here, I'm sure she might try a bit harder."

Shit… Hemi squared his shoulders and kept walking. What came next would be the toughest conversation he'd ever faced.

Chapter Twenty

Hemi wasn't at the mechanics bay. He wasn't at home either. *Where the hell is he?* She'd searched all over town, except the shipping bay, because that wouldn't make sense. She found Jack, who had said last time he saw Hemi headed for the Watering Hole.

Sophia refused to walk back in there with the possibility of running into her parents or Caden being all too real. She refused to talk to them until the morning, when they were leaving. Her last hours in Frog Lick needed to be with Hemi and he wasn't anywhere to be found.

Fuck it, shipping bay it is.

She jumped up from the living room chair and headed for the front door, but before she could reach it, the door sprang open. She jumped, hand to her chest, then saw it was Hemi.

Hemi, who looked as depressed as Gaia had mentioned. His shoulders were hunched. As he took off his sun goggles and lowered his face covering, she saw no smile, no light to his eyes.

"Where have you been?" She sounded panicky, which was annoying, but she couldn't help her worry. The last words he'd shared with her had been devastating.

"Taking care of some business for Drag."

Odd, because the Full Throttle leader had never said as much to her. She considered pressing the issue, but there were more things to be worried about than his location for the last couple hours.

"All right, but you're here now and we need to talk."

Hemi shut the door, locking away the slowly sinking sun and the wind, quieting the room once more. "I thought we shared what needed to be shared in the Watering Hole?"

"Really? Just a simple statement that you don't want to go back and that's supposed to sum up everything. We're bonded." She lifted the sleeve of her shirt up to her shoulder, exposing the tattoo there. The one that symbolized their commitment.

"It's not going to mean anything in two solar days." His voice was so resigned, so emotionless. She fucking hated it, and he wouldn't even look at her. No, he busied himself with removing the sun goggles and hanging them up, with wiping his face down with his cover. Though he added to the insult when he walked off toward the bedroom.

"What are you talking about?" She followed. She had no choice in the matter, because unlike him, she refused to give up. Her belief in fighting for what she wanted, what she loved, ruled above all else. Damn it, she loved him.

"I'm talking about officially telling Drag I'm leaving. I'm damaged goods, can't drive a racer. My mechanic skills are just fine, but compared to Snapper and Gina, I'm a novice. It's time for me to depart Full Throttle. Meaning that tattoo you wear won't have any standing, since I'll no longer be a member of the gang."

No... Her brain rioted, bursting with a million questions and statements. The loudest was the scream gathering at the back of her throat because why? Why was he detonating everything The same way he had when he disappeared in the dead of night in Aurestral ten years prior? With nothing but a shitty note that said *"farewell and good luck."* Four little words for all the time they'd spent together.

The scream faded away at the truth staring her in the face.

"You're running."

Hemi froze for only a split second before heading over to the ion shower. "I'm doing what's best for everyone involved."

He started to strip, and Sophia leaned against the far wall of the washroom as she crossed her arms. "That's a pretty story you tell yourself. Is that the same thing you said when you wrote me that crappy goodbye note before you left Aurestral?"

"That was different." He didn't hesitate in his answer, didn't glance at her as he shucked off his pants. The cybernetic parts gleamed under the overhead lights.

"Explain it to me, because I'd like to know how abandoning me the first time is different from the second."

He turned toward her and glared. *Finally!*

"I'm not abandoning you."

"In the eyes of gang theology, you are. A spouse who walks away is abandonment. You're marking me in a way that can't be redeemed."

"I'm freeing you." He growled.

"I don't want to be free." She uncrossed her arms and stalked toward him, removing her clothes as she went. If this was truly the end, which no fucking way, then she'd be damned if she didn't show him what he was giving up.

"Stop." He warned her, holding up his hand. "That's not what—"

"Oh, yes it is. You want to run, to turn me into some marked woman not worthy of marriage. Because that's how they'll see me." She dropped her shirt to the floor and stood there naked before him.

His gaze trailed from her feet upward, lingering in certain places, until he finally looked her in the eyes. She licked her lips in response because somehow his stare had turned predatory. No resignation there, just desire, hot and inflaming.

"This doesn't change things," he said as he reached for her.

"But we're not done talking either."

She closed the gap first, leaning into his kiss and tracing the seam of his lips with her tongue. He opened immediately, capturing her with his teeth, then teasing the tip with his own. The action was more forceful than what they'd shared in the past. His hands were already moving, one toward her breasts and another between her legs.

He dipped in between her labia, and she moaned as he rimmed her entrance with his fingertips. "You're so fucking wet for me. Just a look and you start dripping," he said, the words rough and ragged between kisses.

"Please."

"Begging already?" He tweaked her nipple as he continued to torture her, never quite entering her with his fingers. "You're going to have to be a little more convincing. How bad do you want me?"

She was aware her arousal had turned desperate enough for her to promise nearly anything, but she found the wherewithal to shut her mouth before she acted reckless. He tempted her again, over and over. Flicking her clit, massaging her breasts, dipping inside her only to pull away before she could bear down.

"You're not answering me and if you don't, then I'll jerk off before I stick my cock inside you."

"You're a sludge-sack. I want you bad enough to tell you I love you, that the idea of never having you fuck me again is near unbearable." He tried to pull back, but she grabbed onto his shoulders and gripped him as hard as she could. "No, I need you to know that my wildest dreams about us together couldn't compare to this, and if you're truly going to give up everything, then I need this last time so I can carry the memory with me for the rest of my life. Because no one, and I mean no one, can fuck me like you, Hemi Finster."

His fingers disappeared then, replaced by his cock. He positioned the thick length between her legs and lifted her up with his cybernetic hand as he guided himself inside her with the other.

She gasped at the forceful way he entered her before he stepped backward into the ion shower and put her back against the wall. His forearms supported her, his hands dug into the butt cheeks. When he began to move, she hissed, "Yes."

This was what she wanted, and she let her head fall against the wall, closed her eyes and gave herself up to the experience. He drove into her slow, letting her feel every part of his give and take. Then his voice rumbled against her chest. "Open your eyes and look at me."

She'd wanted to avoid that. Her confession had left a little morsel of fear in her chest that he wouldn't return those words she'd confessed. That her feelings were too deep, too much for him. But she took a deep breath amidst him plunging deep inside her again, and dared to face him.

The pleasure was so damn acute, so raw and delicious. Already she was halfway to an orgasm and he'd only entered her a minute or two prior. Then she truly saw him. The want, the need, the torture he put himself through reflected back at her. He was taking his time on purpose, when the tension in his frame was so wound she wondered how long he'd last before he snapped.

Watching him this way sent a shudder through her body, and he met that reaction with another slow stroke inside her.

"Fuckkkkkk."

He chuckled and moved again. "You want a memory? Then you're going to have one. We're not leaving this room until you're so weak you can't stand. Until I've marked every inch of you and my cock has left an imprint on your pussy you'll never forget."

Those words paired with his forward motion sent her over the edge. She screamed out his name, and as her cry ended, he whispered harshly in her ear, "I'm not done yet."

She silently thanked whatever deities existed for this because she hoped it would never end.

* * * *

Hemi woke in the middle of the night in a panic. The nightmare had threatened again. The crash, losing control as the flames erupted over his body. The pain and anguish as his nerves were lit up, and the idea of Sophia watching the entire thing...

Except no, she was sleeping next to him. Her body was turned toward him, still naked from their marathon session in the shower. Even with all that, staring at her, recalling her words of love and heartfelt need, he grew hard all over again. She'd brought up some hurtful things that were hard to ignore and other truths he wished he could change, but the future required them to go their separate ways.

The concept of returning to Aurestral, the place he'd tried so hard to escape... That wasn't his dream. He wanted to be the ruler of his future. Now he had a future without racing and how did that happen?

Sophia whimpered and he reached for her, pulling her closer to him and relishing in the way she went so willingly. How she clung to him. It would be hard to give this up. She'd wanted him even when he was falling apart, desired him when he was less than a person and not sure if he would survive.

She'd awakened him, christened him in this new form sexually, and the way her body aligned to his... *Fuck it.* He'd have her again.

Because in the morning he would have to give her up. There was no way she'd change his mind about that. She was as much a part of Aurestral as he wasn't. If he asked, he was sure she would go with him, but to deprive her of her dream... She was born to be a leader, to take charge and to change the world in her own way.

To selfishly prevent that would be wrong, but for the moment, he could at least be a little self-serving. He slid back the sheet, and moved down the bed, putting gentle pressure on her thighs to encourage her to open them.

Her legs stretched open, and he set to work, spreading her lips before he dipped his tongue in to flick her clit. She moved a bit at the sensation, but he wasn't the least bit sorry if this woke her. In fact, he wanted her moaning his name after she woke, the ultimate goal.

She tasted of everything clean and savory, and wholly Sophia. Her arousal coated his tongue as he moved lower, lapping at her sweetness before dipping inside, then out again. He focused on her clit and brought his fingers into play.

Besides the way she arched against him, he could tell she was awake when she put a hand to his head, guiding him where she wanted him.

"Right there...God."

He chuckled and sucked harder on the nub, then plunged two fingers inside her at the same time, pumping as he would with his cock soon enough. The movements were fast, eager, and before he knew it, she was grinding against his mouth and gyrating on his fingers. Insatiable, and he loved how she sought her pleasure, using him like a tool, which was exactly what he could be. A machine for her desire to be unleashed.

Soon she was thrashing against the bed and had released her hold on his head. He put his arm over her hips to keep the lower part of her still enough to finish the job. As her legs locked and her orgasm crested, he lowered himself to receive the gift. There was nothing as glorious as licking away the evidence of what he did to her.

He rose up then, dragging his cock across her entrance, coating himself in whatever remained, then slid home. There was nothing like being inside her. Not from that first time to now. Each experience was as good as the last, if not better. As he started to move, the truth of the future hit. The idea he'd sleep without her, wake without her, live without her.

It only made him want to imprint somehow on her. He leaned down to suck her breasts, hard enough to leave marks. Followed by her neck, low at first, then behind her ears. He'd ensure that everyone knew she belonged to him.

If I can't have her, no one will.

It was an irrational thought when all he needed to do was stay, but the fear of obscurity and living a life once more that had only brought him pain in childhood was impossible for him to contemplate. Even with the temptation of access to her body every day and night. To her jokes and smiles.

"I love it when you fuck me." Her dirty whispers in his ear.

He pounded into her as hard as he dared, loving how she held onto him tightly and pulled his mouth to hers. The dance of their tongues, the gasp as she was nearing her crisis again. How she screamed and he caught the sound. It was enough to send them both over the edge. Him frozen, unable to move, as he came, spilling within her.

It was minutes before she loosened her hold enough for him to roll off her onto his back. He was exhausted all over again, but in the best way. The first rays of sun were starting to peek over the horizon as the room had already lightened enough he could see her a little better.

She was smiling at him. "One helluva way to wake up in the morning. I really—"

"Hold that thought." He pushed off the bed and went to the bathroom, first to relieve himself and gather a cloth so she could clean up. But by the time he turned around, she was already at the door.

"I need the room real quick."

He nodded in agreement and left to give her privacy, opting to go ahead and pull on some pants, along with a sleeveless top. He'd need to pack his duffel today. He surveyed the room. There wasn't much in here that was his besides the items hanging in the small closet. This house had served as a place to rest his head without being exposed to the elements. It was more than what he'd ever had before, yet odd because he didn't own the place.

He would depart the same way he'd arrived—with a single bag of belongings and the clothes on his back. The only question would be if he'd ask Jack for a ride to the nearest gang-town, though he doubted the resources could be spared unless a trade run was happening.

Sophia walked out of the washroom in the middle of his musing and jumped back on the bed. "Why are you dressed? If you're going to live up to your promise from last night, I need you at least twice more."

He would have gladly given her what she wished, though to keep going only delayed what the rising sun guaranteed. "I think it's time we finish that talk."

Facing her, he watched as her smile faded, the brightness in her eyes dulling. She sat up straight before clearing her throat. "Then you haven't changed your mind?"

"Is that what all the sex was for? I won't lie, it's tempting, but if I'm so weak that I'll fall for the first woman who throws herself at me, then you shouldn't want me to begin with."

She pursed her lips and the gaze narrowed on him. "You left out the part where I said I loved you."

The only way I win this is by being heartless. "It's nothing I haven't heard a million times before. I'm good in bed. I was a driver. There are plenty of women who've confessed more than love to me in the bedroom. Some were even willing to handcuff themselves to my bed for an indefinite amount of time if it meant I'd continue to be with them. So, forgive me if those words don't have more of an effect than what you thought they—"

The loud crack of her palm against his cheek was unexpected, and effectively silenced him. Hemi had done his best not to look at her straight on, while fixating on a single point right where her shoulder met her neck.

He deserved her hit, and it stung like hell, but between the fire and his cybernetic surgery... *Don't forget all those lashings you took for her...* He'd suffered enough physical pain.

When she moved to strike him again, he caught her by the forearm. "I understand the urge to lash out with more than words, but I won't be a punching bag. I've done that enough for you in the past, don't you think?"

Her anger crumbled, as did the righteous fury in her eyes, and her straight frame collapsed as she slumped into the mattress and began to cry. He was the biggest asshole of Wespero in this moment, saying the things he did and throwing their past back in her face. *But it's for the greater good.*

He would pay his penance in the years spent away from her, but one day she'd thank him. "I'll head out first. My stuff is already packed. You can leave whenever you're ready. No one will force you out."

"Why are you doing this? You said the past didn't matter."

Hemi sighed as he picked up his duffle bag. "It will, though. My past will influence those around you, and as much as I want to say I'm immune, I'm not. I won't be able to handle the things they will say about you, about me, and I can't sit by and deal with your parents either. They will never accept me. See this for what it is—a chance for you to have the future you want and no negative influence."

She didn't respond and he refused to take the risk of looking at her. The tug on his heart already present. A part of him wanted to give in, but then he'd be submitting himself to a potential future he'd resent.

He stopped at the entrance to the bedroom. "Goodbye, Sophia. I wish you the best."

Chapter Twenty-One

Hemi had left. *He fucking left...*

Sophia swiped the wetness from her cheeks. She refused to shed any more tears. Not after she'd put herself out there and confessed her feelings only for Hemi to throw them back at her.

It didn't take her long to get dressed and assemble her few possessions. She was ready to leave this tiny house which barely had any decent amenities. How silly she'd been, letting herself get caught up in this stupid fantasy to realize she'd settled for very little but sexual gratification.

Hemi ran at the first signs of difficulty. And there's going to be even more trouble.

Her future plans to help Aurestral and partner with Full Throttle would require strength and maneuvering. She didn't trust Caden. Teija might have her back, but could she still put her faith in him?

I don't know.

The risks she'd take now were more than all her childhood adventures combined. She'd risk her very life to pull this off, because if she didn't, no doubt Caden would take everything over and dispose of her.

Without Hemi beside her as leverage with his strength and connection to Full Throttle, she had one other option. *I need to meet with Gaia before I leave.*

* * * *

"Are you ready to get out of this forsaken town, Sophia?" Her mother's question came just as Sophia took a long sip of tea, steeped to perfection moments prior and finally cool enough to drink.

A smartass remark sat on the tip of her tongue, and she did her best to hold it in. She wanted to tell her mother that this town was probably the most successful in all of Wespero and that if anything was forsaken, it was Aurestral. The grandiose walls and buildings within the city were merely a façade. One Sophia intended to strip away, then give Aurestral a true chance to rise from nothing

Instead, play the part.

"Yes, is everyone else ready?"

"Your father and Caden are in a last-minute discussion with the Full Throttle leader. I'm still frustrated that you even suggested this alliance, but if the men believe it worthwhile, then needs must."

With her last sentences, it was like her mother had summoned her father and Caden like some sort of evil mastermind calling forth slithers. Both men appeared out of the hallway and immediately headed toward them.

"Ah, Sophia. You look refreshed and ready to go, is that right?"

Caden's question made her want to roll her eyes. She stopped herself just in time. They had nothing better to talk to her about, it seemed. Only if she was ready to leave. Though she trusted her mother's dislike and animosity of Frog Lick more than she did Caden's smiles. The genial nature he kept on the outside had to be a mask.

Teija had opted to wait with the hauler, choosing to steer clear of as much interaction with Caden and her parents as possible. Until she knew if she could trust him or not, she preferred it. The whole room quieted down as Sophia stood. The group walked out together, and Sophia dared to glance back at Gaia, who remained stoic and more in control than Sophia was.

Tears threatened anew as she tugged her sun goggles in place. She willed herself to stop.

Stay strong.

A tiny sliver of desperation had her glancing around for Hemi as she stepped outside. She'd looked for him everywhere on her way over, hoping behind hope he'd change his mind and pick them. *Pick me.* That maybe he'd already be waiting in the hauler, one of two her parents had brought, specially outfitted with a cover over the back-seat passenger area to allow the riders to remove sun goggles and facial protection.

Privileged rides that typically put more stress on the drivers and... *Maybe he's in there.* Her steps quickened to the hauler Teija stood next to. He opened the door, and she slid into the seat, immediately ripping off her goggles. Her heart pounded in her chest, but it broke again at the empty seat beside her.

"Scoot over if you don't mind, Sophia." Caden spoke softly as he blocked out any remaining light filtering in from the open hauler door. "Your mother wanted to ride with you, but I begged her to give me a chance to speak with you before we arrive in Aurestral."

She did so, if only not to make a scene. This was the part she dreaded, being alone with Caden and having to make nice talk. Sophia would rather be left to her quiet ride, which would allow her to contemplate her next steps even as she also tried her best not to think about Hemi.

As soon as the door shut and they were ensconced in the shade of the cover, Caden turned toward her. "So, your new husband isn't coming?"

"Not yet." Of course, he'd angle for information about Hemi. She was determined to tell no one of how he had ended their relationship. She hadn't even told Gaia or Petal. This would be the secret she'd carry.

"When will he join you?"

"When he's done with his work. There are tasks he has to complete for his debt to Full Throttle, then he will return."

She'd play this game for as long as she could.

Caden sat back, relaxing against the hauler seat cushions, and clicked his tongue against his teeth. "I'm surprised you're that patient. All reports had spoken of the Aurestral princess being demanding in her wants and needs. If you cared for him so much, I'm shocked you didn't appeal directly to the Full Throttle leader to release Hemi to you."

"Wouldn't be very diplomatic if I did. I'm trying to build an alliance, not destroy one. Imagine what the combined might of Aurestral, Full Throttle and Osprerine might accomplish."

"Yes." He stroked his chin and stared out of the shaded window. It was a few moments before he spoke again. "I admire your actions, but doubt this bargain you've made has much to stand on."

"It's barely started. Why do you doubt it?"

Caden turned to face her and grinned. "No particular reason, just forming partnerships with other gangs has always been a bit of a problem. How about we make a bet of it?"

Hell no.

She disliked this man even more. He was revealing exactly the type of person he was, and wagers included, she doubted his ability to lead. Though she needed to know his full plan and drawing him out through conversation was the easiest way.

"What do you suggest?"

"If you can get your father to agree to all the terms and sign an agreement, I'll go away. Back to Osprerine and let you have Aurestral all to yourself. But if I can produce a better opportunity that sways your father's approval, you revoke your binding tattoo and marry me instead."

She opened her mouth. The words about how he didn't even like her sat on the tip of her tongue, but she held them back.

"I don't like how you're not sticking to what we originally discussed, and you know my father will bend easily to your opinions over that of a woman's... There's no easy way for me to succeed."

The smile on Caden's face seemed to grow in size, the arrogance in his eyes apparent. "Then at least you already realize it's futile. Too bad your husband didn't join you, because once we are out of this territory and back in the bosom of your city, I plan to wage war."

"I won't let you win." She clenched her fists against her sides. Her belief was right from the get-go. Caden wanted only one thing, and it wasn't her. In engaging with the women of Full Throttle, they'd made her realize she'd have to fight this battle herself. If she'd learned one thing in Frog Lick, it was that she held more power than this idiot or her father believed.

"You already said you know you can't beat me, so how do you plan to stop me?"

"Like the brewing of ale or the cultivating of crops, you'll just have to wait and see my plans flourish."

She turned away from him, slipped on her sun goggles and pulled up the edge of the shade. She let her gaze focus on the dry desert-like ground they drove through, its random cacti plants, and shrubs dotting the surface with the odd appearance of a goosemert or bob-scratcher on a rock or in the distance chasing prey. A simpler life, still fraught with dangers. Though when faced with the trials she'd undergo next, why would she have preferred to roam free?

* * * *

"You're really going to let her go back to that lion's den all by herself?" Drag's question came as the others stared him down. Jack, Shannon, Gina and Snapper. They'd all gathered in the mechanics bay a week after Sophia had departed. He was there to give his farewells.

"She's following a path I can't be part of. At least not the way I am now."

Snapper made a noise, then grumbled, "And you can't stay here either?"

He'd made that decision the moment he'd walked out of the house he'd shared with Sophia. Since then, he'd been crashing where he took physical therapy. Shannon was probably well aware, but she hadn't called him on it.

"You're family, Hemi." Gina stood up straight, no longer leaning against Snapper's frame. "Just like

Shannon, like me. You may not have started here, but you belong."

Jack chimed in, along with Shannon, Drag and Rune, who'd just arrived, with similar sentiments of agreement.

Damn if those words of support and camaraderie didn't hit him straight in the chest. He rubbed at his sternum, as if it might clear some of the pain. This was similar to the ache he'd experienced watching the hauler holding Sophia pull out of Frog Lick.

He'd wanted to go to her, the same way he wanted to speak words that would reassure Drag and the others, but he decided to opt for the truth.

"I'm never going to race again."

Everyone fell silent at his confession.

"We didn't make your entry into Full Throttle contingent on you needing to."

"Kind of figured after the other day." Jack's response came at the same time as Drag's.

Then Gina added, "Shannon already warned us there might be some issues that wouldn't be fixed with physical therapy and that's okay."

"Black holes you all are," Shannon hollered. "Can't you see it's part of his identity? If he can't do that, what good is he? That'd be like Snapper being unable to work on racers or Gina unable to solve complex mathematical equations or Jack... Well, I'll keep that to myself."

Hemi shook his head. "You're a dirty one, Shannon."

"I aim to please, but what you're saying Hemi, I understand it. The same as any of us no longer being able to do what we're good at. But it doesn't mean you need to sleep on a weight bench instead of your own bed. Doesn't mean you need to punish yourself by leaving. Besides, where the hell will you go?"

He still wasn't sure. "Figured I might wander a bit. The racing domes always need workers, they might take in a temporary."

"Dome work? Are you serious?" Snapper scoffed. "You want to dig in and debase yourself, we have sanitation and waste processing jobs here. You don't have to travel to learn a new trade."

Hemi wanted to be able to leave before they discovered he was worthless, before they could decide to abandon him. "Listen, I'm not good at the long haul. Drag, I told you as much when you let me test run for you. Sticking around, family-type environments…I've always been on my own and it's better for me to get out now before I let you all down even more."

"You mean, before you run the risk of getting hurt?" The voice who spoke wasn't one of the others and Hemi glanced up to see Gaia standing there, her arms crossed, a deep frown on her face.

"That's not—"

"Save the excuses. You wounded Sophia pretty bad. She came to me with a strong act, but I knew she was hurting. Seems you like to make sure those who care about you suffer because you're afraid. But with us, you don't have to be."

How he wished those words were true. "A gang is only as strong as the pieces within. That's what was ingrained in me. Even if you were the best, though, it didn't mean anyone truly cared for you or deemed you worthy."

"When was the first time they told you that you weren't going to matter to them? When did Papal tell you that you would never be with Sophia?"

Gaia's questions rooted Hemi to the floor. He couldn't move… *Hell, can't breathe*. The memories were like the fire in the racer all over again, burning him alive as they rose to the surface. "I don't—I can't talk about then."

"You should, because you let those Aurestral bastards make you believe this spaced idea you would never be enough, that you couldn't be appreciated for who you are, and wanting anything more only meant heartache. You came here seeking a future away from the negativity, and when it didn't work as planned, you chose to go right back to running…the way you ran from Sophia before."

Gods, his chest was tight. Maybe his heart had stopped working right, or the nanites malfunctioned. "I can't breathe."

"Shit." Shannon rushed to his side. "There might be a problem with his components."

"There's nothing wrong with him." Gina's voice seemed distant and emotionless. "His cybernetics are fully operational. Whatever he is experiencing is self-induced, mentally."

"Do you love her, Hemi?" Gaia wouldn't let up.

"I—why does it matter?"

"Matters a whole lot when you sent her away to face enemies all by herself. Thought we taught you better than that," Drag replied.

They stood there accusing him, judging him for the choices he'd made. All for the safety of himself and the idea of Sophia in danger. *Fuck*. He pounded a fist on his chest, willing himself to calm down, to find some calm.

The memories of being hailed as unworthy, unable to be a candidate for Sophia were there in the forefront. How all the beatings he'd suffered had destroyed his hope for the one day they would be together. So, he chose to leave, to run from her. If he couldn't have her, why be near her?

If he couldn't have racing, why stay?

"I don't want to lose anything else I love. There! I said it. I love her. I loved racing. I can't stand to watch the things I care about most be stripped from me."

Hemi glanced at his companions expecting the worst, but instead he found Jack smiling. Shannon was a bit teary-eyed as she hovered near him. Gina was impassive as always, but she gripped Snapper's arm tight. Drag shook his head, the only one besides Gaia looking at him like he was stupid.

Gaia spoke next. "The worst thing a person can do is let the ones they love suffer needlessly. Hands down, up or any which way. We may not be perfect here in Full Throttle, but we believe in ensuring those we care for don't have pain."

The dark chuckle that escaped Hemi came from a place of hurt, for being called out like this. "Well, if that was your plan, you didn't do too well when you saved me."

Drag stepped forward. "You're still angry about that, and it was my fault. Selfishly, I wanted to save you. So did Snapper, Jack and Rune."

"I did," Rune muttered from behind his brother.

"We were willing to do whatever to keep you alive. Our own guilt ate at us, but looking back, while it may not have been the best choice, I do believe installing cybernetics in you was the right move. You can hate me if you want, but you alive today means you can love Sophia tomorrow."

The words rang with a bitter truth. If they'd left him to die, then there would be no marriage to Sophia, no confirmation she loved him. His stupid decisions to spare her from his uncertain future were merely symbolic of his inability to let the past go and be the person he'd been since the day he'd set foot in Frog Lick.

"I've already made too many mistakes. Not sure I can take some of them back."

Gaia came over and wrapped her arms around him in a hug. "The only mistake I can see is you let her leave. There's still time to get her back."

The others started to pile in, murmuring words of equal sentiment.

"Yeah, and groveling is a great way to get her back."

"Or just confess your love."

"Maybe try to be there for her. That goes a long way."

"Does this mean you're still leaving Frog Lick?" The last question from Rune came as they all hugged Hemi then slowly took a few collective steps backward, each person letting go of the embrace.

When Hemi was on his own again, he took in a deep breath as he looked into the eyes of the ones he could truly call family. He'd been so locked up by the past, consumed by Sophia's arrival and the unbidden memories of failure and rejection she'd brought with her, that he'd forgotten the person he'd become here. How those in Full Throttle had shaped him and made him strive to be a better version of himself. Through love, through caring and general decency that other territories and gangs lacked in general.

Why can't I help Sophia bring the same thing to Aurestral that Drag has done for Full Throttle? He might not race, but he could be an instrument of change.

"Yes, I'll have to leave because that's the only way to win back my wife."

The whoops and cheers from the others echoed through the mechanics bay, though the appearance of

Rune's wife Petal brought everyone to silence. Petal's skin was flushed from running, her chest heaving as she took in breaths.

"What's wrong, love?" Rune asked, stroking Petal's back.

"We've just received this from Aurestral with our latest hauler return. There was a coup in Aurestral."

Chapter Twenty-Two

Sophia was exhausted. She only needed a few more days, maybe a week, and everyone would be in place. Enacting the plan she'd concocted with Gaia and Petal before her departure hadn't been as hard as she'd thought. Not with the women of the Frog Lick Social Club so eager to help if it meant freeing others from servitude and bonds of injustice, as Yuma had put it.

The days and nights were long, with messages conveyed through covert channels. She even had to reluctantly bring Teija into the fold, though she kept her details scarce around him. Slowly but surely, those women who'd arrived in Aurestral set up work, spreading news of the alliance with Full Throttle, of the plans for education in food production, improvements being proposed for better water systems and waste management. For general growth among the people, not set to classes. Interest was high, even as skepticism spread with equal fervor. People wanted change but found it difficult to truly believe it was coming.

Armed with the people's wishes, with plans and costs from all her research, Sophia found herself at dinner that night ready to confront her father with her ideas. Whether Caden would support them remained unknown. He'd been working his own goals since their arrival, but every evening found some way to ask about Hemi. Relentless was the best word to describe Caden's pursuit of information about her marriage.

And it's exhausting.

"When will your husband join us?" He smiled sweetly, as if he wasn't a slither slyly attempting to infiltrate everything her family had built here and take it for himself.

"Soon. I have word he plans to join us with the next shipments." A lie she'd keep selling. She'd said the same days ago. "Father, speaking of next shipments, I'd also like to talk about some ideas I have for continued improvements. With Marsanium populating our city again, we can begin to get back to the ship work. To move away from the trades we've engaged in and start educating our people. The men will need support from a food perspective and I believe Frog Lick has tactics — "

"You really expect Hemington to come here?" Her mother cut her off, and Sophia wanted to growl with frustration. Especially with how her mother liked to use Hemi's full name every time she brought him up now.

"Yes, I would plan for my husband to be here with me as we help usher Aurestral into a bright new future."

"What about Caden? He has plans, too." Her mother took a sip of wine and nodded toward the man in question.

Caden's wide grin was the fakest smile she'd ever beheld. "I do have plans. Though they may not be as people-serving as Sophia's. I'm afraid mine are a little more self-serving."

If she'd hadn't been raised to display impeccable manners, Sophia's mouth would have dropped open. He'd as well as admitted to not giving a single shit about their gang-town. Yet her parents were still determined to entertain this fool.

"Nothing wrong with worrying about your future and setting things in motion to protect it before moving on to more charitable projects," her father said.

"Indeed." Caden lifted his glass. "That's why I propose a toast. To both you, Papal and your fair wife, for offering me a place here."

Everyone took deep gulps from their glass, except Sophia.

"And to a future that I can be secure in." Caden raised his glass again and her parents joined in. Sophia motioned with the glass but didn't drink.

No, she refused to play into this celebration of stupidity. *Three more days, then we begin.*

"I say, Sophia—" Metal clattered against metal and her father suddenly pitched forward, his head hitting the table with a loud thud and the food splattering everywhere. A speck of the meal hit her cheek.

She gasped and glanced to her mother, who let out a squeak then did the same movement, though over the side of her chair as she'd moved toward her husband in his distress.

"What did you do?" Sophia asked, tears flooding her eyes. Her parents…she had no clue if they were dead or alive, but she immediately tossed the glass of wine away from her. Her stomach soured at the realization that something had been put in their drink.

"The only thing a jilted man can do when his fiancée steals the gang he was going to gain — get rid of the obstacles to succession."

"Since I didn't drink your poison, do you mean to kill me with other means?"

He laughed and drank from his glass again, polishing off what remained before wiping away any evidence of the red wine from his lips with his sleeve. "So dramatic. Nothing drastic for you. I need you to make this legitimate. If you behave as well, I'll even let you wander back to your sludge-sack lover if he means that much to you."

"Kind of difficult to marry you when I'm already bound to someone else." She was doing her best to stay still and to keep the tears she wanted to shed at bay. She had to assess the threat. There was no way to be sure he was sincere in his decision to marry her.

"Easy enough to remedy. I'll have the tattoo removed."

Removed? Such a thing involved an extremely painful process.

"If I refuse?"

"Then consider everything you're trying to make happen over. I can take the gang-town by force, but it's not as appealing and the commission may question it. Or you can abandon your driver, marry me and continue with your little pet projects after I take over the bulk of the setup here."

She glanced again at her parents and wanted to scream her outrage. Agony at how they'd never seen this building. Their demise had been so simple when they thought they were trading for a future. Though she was sad, her heart aching for the people who had raised her, even as they'd tried to sell her off for their own gain, a part of her knew they would have never backed her plans anyway.

But I have allies.

There were people in place. When news got out to Full Throttle about her parents... *He might come for me.* At least she needed to believe that to say what she needed to next.

"Can I have time to decide?"

Caden pushed out of his chair to a standing position and approached her. "A day? Two? Would you be inclined to consider faster if I kissed you?"

This man made her stomach churn. While gorgeous with sun-kissed locks, stormy blue eyes and penchant for keeping his cheeks free of any facial hair, he had no soul. Not with his bloodthirsty desire for power and his inability to be faithful to anyone.

"Let's save the kiss for my decision in two days."

It wasn't the three she needed, but it would have to do, because now her goal had changed from pushing reform to starting a rebellion.

* * * *

The word of Papal and his wife's death spread quickly throughout Frog Lick. The assassination was all anyone talked about. At least to Hemi, it felt like the main topic of conversation. From the moment he'd been handed the letter Petal had received, time had moved in slow motion. He'd wanted to leave that very moment, steal a hauler... *Hell, a racer.* He'd been halfway to getting inside one before Jack stopped him.

"We don't have a plan yet, brother."

The sentence sobered him enough to get him calm, but he was still far from okay.

I let her leave not caring for the danger she'd be in.

Not realizing how much jeopardy he'd put her in. Since that moment, Drag and the others had sprung into action. Now they'd gathered in the back room of the Watering Hole to discuss the findings and Hemi was one shaky breath away from throwing things.

There was so much nervous energy coursing through him he barely noticed everyone filing into the room.

Gaia was the last one in. "Sorry, had to give instructions to the girls for the meal tonight. I'm not used to being away during serving time."

"We thank you for helping us because it appears you know more about what Sophia has going on than anyone else."

Hemi's attention caught on Sophia's name, and he shoved himself to a standing position. "What about Sophia? What does she know?"

"It's a bit complicated, but it might help to say that there are people from Frog Lick already in place within the limits of Aurestral."

Drag's frown deepened. "How many?"

"At least half a dozen women who can be trusted to infiltrate and assimilate into groups without bringing attention to the fact they aren't from the area." Gaia held out her hands as if trying to invoke a sense of calm through a room of men who were anything but. "Drag, for all you talk about trusting the womenfolk to business matters and believing in our ability to be as intelligent as the rest of you, this bit of misogyny filtering through the room needs to stop. I wouldn't send anyone into a situation they couldn't handle. Yuma, Artie and Michelle plus a few others are perfectly capable of quelling drunks, starting fights themselves and battling off unwanted advances."

The words worked. Even Hemi felt a bit chastised at the fact he'd been so eager to believe Sophia under threat to the point she couldn't survive without him. She'd made it ten years with him gone, and she had Teija if she truly needed help. *Though why Teija didn't protect her parents doesn't make sense.*

"Fine. You're right, Gaia. But I won't apologize for being worried about the people who entrusted me with their care."

Gaia smiled. "I wouldn't try to take that away from you either. Just no glowering. Now, Sophia's idea was to gain the ear of the people of Aurestral. To sway their opinions so that they would openly support her ideas to implement some of the same practices we have here in Frog Lick. In three days' time, myself and Petal would have joined her and worked to begin teaching those in Aurestral in different departments, from gardening with airponics to the hydroponics work that Artie is well-versed in. Except I imagine this Caden wants nothing to do with those ideas in truth."

Gina cleared her throat. "That's where I would agree with you. Caden's name pops up in Bridget's files we stole when we rescued Jack. Seems this Osprerine heir isn't the first in line. He appealed to Bridget for a marriage before pursuing a similar agreement with Sophia."

A crunch sounded and all eyes went to Drag, who held a crushed can in his hand.

"But," Gina paused for a moment, "Bridget turned him down. He's wanting a place to rule and will basically attempt to steal it from anyone he can, but he's not dumb. The Mars Commission won't let leaders be overthrown. It would start too many inter-gang wars."

Jack scoffed. "We're already at war with Macintosh."

"Yes, but not in their eyes." Gina tossed a holo-screen to the center of the table and activated it, projecting a map of the three regions. "There are several factions warring with others. Near constant, but they keep their battles secret. No big fusses, no coup takeovers. Send assassins, steal some things, as long as they fly under the commission's general big no-no's, then it's a free-for-all."

"How does killing Sophia's parents change things?" Snapper asked as he leaned over the table and used his fingers to zoom in on the location of Aurestral. "He has no allies nearby. Hell, Aurora is a foreign territory."

"He'll marry her." Shannon's announcement made Hemi's blood boil.

"Not possible," he growled. "She's married to me."

"But you're not there, are you?" Gina pressed a button and the map disappeared, replaced by some lines related to gang marriage contracts. "According to this, a married couple is bound by the tattoos they receive. The only way the marriage is voided is if the tattoo is sundered."

"You mean burned from her flesh." Rune offered up this blunt explanation and a couple of the others hissed.

Drag glanced at Hemi and he couldn't look back. Didn't dare to because all he saw at the moment was his failure to do the one thing he'd promised Sophia their marriage would bring — protection.

"Caden kills the parents, the only ones who could stand in the way of him blackmailing or coercing Sophia. He'll torch the damn bonding tattoo off her and make his claim legitimate by placing his in its place." Shannon's recitation of the obvious speared Hemi. He was in that car burning all over again and again.

"No," he yelled as he shook his head. "Over my dead body will I let anything happen to her. We'll invade Aurestral, kill this bastard Caden."

Jack waved his hand in the air. "And?"

"What?"

"You're going to tell her you love her, right?"

Hemi gave a half-hearted laugh. "We're talking about the future of an entire gang, about Sophia being tortured, and you're worried about when I'll declare my feelings for her? You're a dumbass."

"No, I want to make sure you're thinking about all the important things."

"It's true," Rune added. "He's right."

The others began to talk amongst themselves. Hemi kept the rest of his thoughts inside.

Yes, of course he fucking planned to tell Sophia how he felt once they made sure she was safe. No way in hell he'd leave her side again. He'd been an idiot in the first place and the mere idea of her getting hurt all because she'd married him was unacceptable. He would fix this, then make sure no one ever tried to hurt her again.

"What else do we need to be worried about, Gina?" This came from Drag, who'd been eerily quiet outside of his outburst toward the idea of Bridget marrying.

Gina pressed another button pulling up some communication logs between Macintosh and Osprerine. "They do have an accord to come to each other's aid. Appears we weren't the only ones with ideas around making allies. Though it's minor, Osprerine was originally chatting about an alliance years prior to Bridget taking over as leader. Since then, the Osprerine leader stupidly put Caden as the responsible party for building the relationship. He's made a poor bargain, but it's one that, with a simple message, Macintosh would send at least a couple haulers with people with the intention of disruption."

"Fuck." Snapper's sentiment most likely mirrored everyone else's thoughts.

"It can't be easy, can it?" Jack offered this up along with a bottle of some fine mash he'd pulled from a box somewhere. He twisted off the cap and brought the bottle to his lips. "Means we can't risk leaving Frog Lick unguarded."

Jack swallowed a good amount then began passing the bottle. Each of the others took a drink, even Gina. Gina must have been concerned because she rarely imbibed.

"You're right. We can't afford to give Bridget a chance to attack us here. At the same time, we have to help our ally too. We can—"

"Send me by myself." Hemi's statement came right as Shannon handed the bottle to him. He took it and poured a good swallow into his mouth. The damn shit, even of a higher quality, still burned. Though the warmth it spread through his limbs was worth it.

"I'm not going to let you go off alone when the rest of us—"

"He won't be alone." Gaia walked around the table and over to Hemi's side where she took the bottle next. "I'll go with him."

Drag frowned. "Do I ever get to speak a full sentence again or—"

"What?"

"Fuck you, Rune."

Everyone let out a chuckle at that. Hemi found the moment a nice little sidetrack from the truth of what he'd said. He fully meant it, though. He'd go alone to Aurestral if needed and take this task on himself.

"Gaia, I'm not doubting your abilities, but Frog Lick can't lose you."

The woman smiled, little dimples on her cheeks clearly visible and making her look younger. "I won't be gone forever, you charmer. I know it's my cooking you'll miss, but I promised Sophia. Besides, you are the one, along with the others here, that can't leave Frog Lick. You need to present a strong and united front. Prepare for the race, because with Hemi's departure and Jack's retirement, there's only one person left to lead us to the finish line."

"You sure about this?" Shannon asked Hemi, reaching out to touch his cybernetic arm. The warmth radiated through him.

"Yeah, I owe her this much. I can handle myself. If you can spare Gaia so she can guide me through Sophia's plan, and maybe we take a couple of the other ladies, too…anything to lower their guard. I think we stand a chance."

The looks of concern didn't disappear as the bottle began to make the rounds again.

"I could go," Gina offered, but Snapper clamped a hand over her mouth.

"Nope, out of the question. You could, but we're already risking Gaia."

"And me," Petal chimed in. She'd been awfully quiet entering the room. "There's another message from Aurestral, this from Teija. We're out of time."

Chapter Twenty-Three

Sophia woke to a red dawn. They weren't frequent and she'd heard dozens of myths about what such a foreboding visual meant.

That death would come, the signal of danger, of change or of violence. Whatever connotation she used meant that after today, things wouldn't be the same. She had to give her decision, but she was sure that no matter what she said to Caden, he'd still burn the symbol of her bond to Hemi from her arm.

Caden would force his own binding tattoo upon her skin and kill her if she didn't agree. She hugged her pillow to herself and fell back to the mattress, hot and fresh tears pouring down her face.

Her parents were dead, and the grief was still so new. After the shock had worn off, she'd realized Teija hadn't come to her aid. No, her bodyguard had stood outside that room barring all others from entering. Whatever hold Caden had over him was strong enough to earn his betrayal.

She cried for the loss of her mother, her father and Teija. No doubt he'd told Caden her plans as well and confessed to knowing Hemi would never come. She was alone, except for the women from Frog Lick out in the city, and she had no way to reach them. Word might have spread. Such big events wouldn't go completely unnoticed.

A knock sounded on her door, then it opened.

Maybe I'm out of time already.

"Sophia, it's me." Teija's voice was no longer a balm of comfort. It was a dagger, come to slice away at her very soul.

"Go away. Unless you were sent to bring me for torture."

"You're so damn dramatic." He slammed the door behind him entering the room, she didn't look, but heard the clomp of his footsteps as he came closer. "Not even going to look at me?"

"Why? So, I can see your betrayal again. You just stood outside while he murdered them. Did you know?"

"He was forced to do that. His father made him. You don't understand what his life is like, the pressure he faces with his family. This was the only way to avoid being punished." Teija's words were so matter-of-fact that Sophia couldn't help but let her jaw drop.

She was shocked beyond belief that somehow Teija believed Caden was helpless. Anyone capable of killing multiple people to get the results they wanted was far from being innocent in any of this.

"Murder is acceptable then?"

Teija frowned at her. "Your parents have done far worse. How many families have been split, children orphaned, me included? I lost mine to the drugs and the trade. My father a dancer, my mother sold as an indentured servant. They weren't good people. Even you have confessed as much over the years. In a way, he did you a favor, got rid of them without you having to live with the guilt."

Tears blurred her vision anew. She was truly mystified at how Teija could be so hoodwinked by this person intent on doing whatever he could for his own selfish purposes.

"No, they weren't perfect. But neither am I. Neither are you. We all do the best we can with the situations we're presented with. I could have worked on my parents. I was working to change their minds about the clubs, the selling of our people and the orphans. Trying to fix things so other children wouldn't have to go through what you and Hemi did."

"Caden will do the same thing, though. He just wants a place to be safe. You agree to this, and he'll let you make the changes you want. I asked him and he made me a promise."

She scoffed. "Like you can trust a word that comes out of his mouth. In Frog Lick, you said you couldn't trust him."

"I overreacted. I was angry because he still wanted to marry you, when he said he loved me. But I wasn't looking at things right."

Holy fuck, her closest friend was brainwashed, and it wouldn't matter what she said. He was convinced this fool loved him. He believed that Caden would really keep her alive after he got what he wanted.

"I'm not going to do it."

Teija sighed, and stepped closer. Only then did she notice he had a syringe in his hand. "You're my friend, Sophia. We're almost like siblings, though not quite because, let's be honest, I always had to ultimately do what you said. But still…I don't want you to die. You have good ideas. You deserve good things."

"Get the hell away from me," she replied, scooting to the edge of her bed and glancing around to see how she could possibly run. He was between her and the door. She might not be able to escape, but damn it.

I'm going to try.

She stood up and he paused, waiting for her to move.

"This can be quick, Sophia. We'll keep you sedated through the procedure. The pain will be minimal."

He's ridiculous.

"Have you ever had your flesh burned away? I don't think so. You can't promise this won't hurt. You can't say anything that will make me believe I'll be okay after this."

She readied herself to try to dash around him, not sure if she'd be successful. *Here's hoping word has reached Frog Lick.*

If not, even if so…she had to have hope. "Sorry, Teija. I don't know what happened to you, but if this is what love does to a person, I want no part of it."

Jetting forward, she darted left, then right, trying her best to not give him an opportunity to anticipate her moves. She grabbed onto one of the sheer fabrics that hung from the top of her bed and pulled as she ran. A good hard yank brought the canopy setup crashing down toward Teija.

It worked and his focus went to the falling upper bed frame as she made it to the door. She threw open the heavy lacquered wood panel and was almost across the threshold when something tugged on her shirt. Then there was a prick on her skin.

She stopped to glance and saw the needle sunk into her upper arm. "Fuck you, Teija. If I live from this, just know we're not friends anymore."

He yanked the needle out of her arm. "I'm sorry you feel that way."

"I do. You're…a…bastard." Each word came out of her and the world felt sloshy, slippery as if she were caught in some sort of soupy fog. Her eyelids got heavy, and she stumbled forward.

Then she was falling toward the ground. Her body would be hurt when she hit. She tried to move her arms, but nothing. This was loss of control. The inability to stop herself from becoming a victim.

Is this how Hemi felt when the racer exploded?

Had he experienced the same desperate desire to be anywhere but in the moment, unable to do anything to change it? She owed him an apology for not having more empathy. For dismissing his preference to keep himself from ever feeling that way again.

She prepared to hit and instead Teija caught her hand. *The bastard.*

"Just relax, Sophia. The tattoo will be removed soon."

Then everything went dark.

* * * *

The sun was setting as they reached the outskirts of Aurestral. The town was more than that—it was a city, thanks to its ten-foot walls built from Marsanium ore and mud.

Hemi vaguely recalled being told how the first of those who called themselves the Aurestral gang set up by beginning the building of the north wall. Then after a couple years, the west wall, followed by east, then south. Within ten years, the buildings and architecture of Aurestral had been admired and envied by other gangs.

But, thanks to the tall structure and the placement of only two gates, no one could penetrate to the inside, unless said person had knowledge of the secret tunnels built for emergencies.

Hemi told Gaia as much on their approach.

"Are you sure this is the best way?" She rode behind him on the uni-rider they'd borrowed from Shannon and Jack. The damn thing worked as a two-seater and was better to travel in than a hauler. Less noticeable too.

"Yeah. We need to get inside without alerting all the guard faction. Connect with Artie and Yuma. You said you know where they are."

"Well, having a note with some names is way different than firsthand experience living here."

"That's why you got me."

On the west edge of Aurestral was a fair-sized forest, a couple dozen acres of land, where he planned to hide the uni-rider. When he got the women from Frog Lick out, they could pick it up then.

"We're almost to the woods. When we get there, prepare to help me find some brush to cover this with."

The lighting within the city gave off a haze that hovered over the walls and illuminated the night sky with yellow. He found he'd missed this part of the place he'd once called home because no matter what time of day, he never felt like he was in the dark.

Though the small memory brought on darker ones. Because for every nice thought he had about this place, there was plenty of cruelty too. They were in the forest before he could get too deep in his maudlin thoughts.

He brought the uni-rider to a halt, and Gaia hopped off, immediately getting to work searching for fallen branches. There were plenty since bob scratchers and yotis wandered the area.

Hemi moved a little slower, inspecting the surroundings for any signs that people were frequenting the place, but his search for tracks revealed nothing.

"Could use a little help with these," Gaia whispered as she tugged on two thicker branches with a fair amount of off-shoots and leaves still attached.

He marched over and took one from her hands. "Got it. I'll place this one first, you grab our supplies off the rider."

Gaia dropped the branch with enthusiasm and unlatched the two duffels they'd secured for the trip, along with the two water skins and a pair of thermal binocs Gina had given him. Though she'd made Hemi promise he'd send them back to her.

"Ready," Gaia said as she draped the straps of the skins around her neck. Her long hair was bundled up against her head in twin buns.

He laid the branch over the back half of the rider before moving to take the other branch from Gaia to cover the front.

"I had that."

"Yeah, but you have the binocs. Take a peek at the entrance to the north and the south for me while I finish this up." He left out the part where he wasn't quite ready to face his past again. Though he needed to push beyond his fears.

Sophia needs you.

She did. There was no time to turn scurdy now.

"All right. See you at the tree line shortly." Gaia pulled her hood over her head and started walking. Her footsteps were quiet, rather like the woman herself. She'd proven a good travel companion and not afraid of any task. He enjoyed that she was the one with him instead of Drag or the others.

Though his task was complete a little sooner than he preferred. He made his way toward Gaia. She was right where she said she'd be, at the tree line, leaning against a tree trunk with the binocs obscuring her vision.

"There are at least six guards on a rotation. Timing it, there is at least one able to spot us every ten minutes. Not much time to move across this distance."

Hemi wasn't surprised the bartender had already figured out the schedule. Hell, it appeared this woman had a lot of hidden talents, like so many of them in Frog Lick. Like Sophia.

"Then I take it you noted the rocks between there and here. Two people can't fit behind them, but one can. We'll move slow. It will take us a little over an hour, but we can get to the wall. They believe in height, not warning systems. Not like those paranoid gangs, Singh or Barnabas. We just hit the wall and from there I can show you the tunnel."

"How can something be such a big secret and then so well-known?"

"Most people have heard of it, but only a few bother to believe in it. It's like telling someone you care for them over and over, then turning around and beating them every day. Can't believe in their feelings when they show you otherwise."

Gaia lowered the binocs. "Is that what they did to you?"

"In a variety of ways, yes. It was always worse when they caught me with Sophia. The damn woman never knew how to stay away from me and deep down I didn't want her to. Even though the cost was so damn high."

"You love her. You finally said so back in the Watering Hole."

"Yeah." Warmth spread in his chest at the memory of her smile, her passion, the way she'd clung to him in the night.

"Then tell me, why do those who love always aim to hurt? Why is it only the threat of death that would get you charging toward here?"

Whatever heat blooming within him went cold. Gaia wasn't wrong, and he harbored some guilt over his hesitance. "I was scared. Scared of this place." He pointed toward the city. "My worst days and nights were here. I can't forget that. I thought I'd be submitting to more pain by coming back. But I realized if something happens to her…"

"You'll be in pain forever anyway." Gaia nodded as she held the binocs out to him. "Then your time to take a peek. Check my timing. If you find it right, we move. Let's go save your woman."

Chapter Twenty-Four

People were speaking around her. She wasn't in her room. There was the heavy scent of jasmine and another heady scent. She'd been falling. Teija had caught her, except he had betrayed her too.

Sophia tried to move her arms, but she'd been rendered immobile. Opening her eyes slowly, she blinked several times to clear away the haze, but it remained. Incense…she'd heard of such things before. Many used the compacted cones filled with scent to chase away other smells.

She glanced toward her right arm, but the tattoo remained, though the sleeve of her top had been cut away to reveal the matrimonial symbol. So much for her being knocked out for this, waking before the procedure had even begun.

"You said you would marry her and let her live."

Caden clicked his tongue against his teeth. "That was if she agreed to my terms. You're telling me she ran. You had to drug her to get her here. Better to just kill her and take the gang by force at this point. I can get Bridget with Macintosh to provide support while I get things set up. She'll love it if I break off the deal with Full Throttle and keep all that ore as well."

If Teija couldn't see this klog's true form with these words, Sophia was at a loss on how to save her once trusted friend. She couldn't believe he'd actually drugged her.

"But the people won't follow. They won't respect your position of authority. It leaves room for another gang to think Aurestral is weak. To believe they can assume control of the city. Not to mention the commission."

Caden reached out and stroked Teija's cheek. "You think I didn't anticipate that? I've met with leaders from Azurite, Gemino and Dawning. They were all tired of the Archers with their noses stuck so far in the air. As if having possession of these walls made them better than anyone else."

So, this wasn't just a random act. Caden had been planning this for a while.

Sophia forced herself to stay quiet, even as she wanted to scream. The names she had for this sludge-sack were so numerous, the curses would have made her dead mother faint. If she was free, and had a weapon of some sort, the torture she'd impart could never be enough to make up for the pain he'd caused.

Thankfully, his attention was fully on Teija with his back to her.

She tested the strength of her restraints. The straps against her legs were looser than those belting her arms to the chair.

"How long have you been planning this?" Teija's question was met with a lyrical laugh.

Caden's voice echoed through the room. The same damn room where he'd killed her parents the two days prior.

"Does it matter? What does is that soon there will be no need for pretenses. I can be with you, and no one will stop us. You should be happy about that. No more needs to throw tantrums about not getting to have me openly." Caden leaned up to kiss Teija and her bodyguard held the other man at a distance.

There was a commotion outside the dining room doors. Sophia could hear shouts, the trample of feet.

Was that a shot fired?

Teija kissed Caden then, and Sophia used the distracting moment to use all the strength she could summon to try to loosen the straps. They barely budged.

Fuck.

Then the doors burst open, and the smell of smoke came first, followed by the unmistakable glimmer of light reflecting off metal.

"Hemi!"

"Hemi!" Sophia shouting his name was music to his ears.

Though it ruined his entrance and the distraction. Caden immediately stepped away from Teija, the pair of them blocking his view of Sophia. The man he wanted to shoot could easily move and he might hit her.

Damn.

The ladies were almost done with their job, though they'd need to put out the fire that had started fairly quickly.

Hemi marched further into the room, pulling a knife from his belt as he stepped forward and threw it in Teija's direction, nailing the bastard in the thigh. "That's for not protecting her from this sludge-sack."

He pulled another knife, then heard Sophia shout, "Get away from me. Don't touch me. The fu —"

"Shut up, or I slice your throat and your half-man, half-machine monster over there can see if tears are compatible with all the electronic hardware he has."

His visual acuity was dampened by the floating incense smoke that hovered throughout the room, but his senses were heightened thanks to the nanites. He could still pick up Caden's movements, the creak of the pressure of his weight against the back of the chair Sophia was strapped to. The strain of leather against wood as she struggled against her bonds with no luck.

"I'm sorry, Hemi. Afraid I have the upper hand here." Caden seemed to enjoy hearing himself talk.

"How so? The guards are dead, the ones that wanted to fight. Most surrendered when we proposed we were here to free their rightful gang leader." Hemi took a step to the right, keeping his gun trained on Caden's head. The sight would work perfect. The laser beam moved faster than old-school bullets. Another gift from Gina, one he was also supposed to return.

"Yes, but I have your loved one. Before you can fire a shot, I'll sever a major artery. You know how fast a human can bleed out?"

"Afraid not. But I know how quickly fuel is dropped from a racer if you cut a line. Sure they're comparable."

Caden chuckled. "Do you even care about her? Seems you know more about racers. We could cut a deal. You support me as the ruler, and I'll let you run the mechanics bay. You can design racers, select drivers. Build your own championship crew."

This idiot, for a genius mastermind, appeared to be pretty dumb where Hemi was concerned.

"Afraid that's not a major way to motivate me anymore. Five years ago, I would have gladly taken your offer. So, you showed up here a little too late. But if you're determined not to let her out of that chair alive, then I have one thing I need to say." Hemi took a deep breath, preparing to bare his soul before he tried to rescue the love of his life.

"Sophia, I love you. I should have never let you walk away from me without telling you that. I should have been braver and willing to face any number of my fears to be with you. For this, I'll spend my life making up my mistake."

Caden sneered. "She'll be dead. Not sure how you repay a dead woman."

Right then a knife flew through the air and the hilt hit Caden's hand. The blond idiot let out a yelp and the knife he'd held to Sophia's throat clattered to the ground.

"I'm sorry, Sophia," Teija said as he fell toward the floor. "Afraid my aim is off."

The action was enough to send Hemi into attack mode. He trained the sight on Caden's forehead and pulled the trigger. His cybernetic arm and hand didn't fail as the laser erupted from the aperture and ended Caden's life in seconds.

Sophia squealed as the dead man hunched over her. Thankfully, the high heat from the laser had cauterized the wound it created, so no blood or brains leaked onto her. Hemi put the gun in its holster and made it to Sophia's side. It wasn't much effort to toss Caden's body across the room. The sound of shattering wood confirmed the dead man had landed.

He easily snapped the leather straps holding her in the chair and reached down to gather her up in his arms. "Thank Mars."

"I can't believe you're here," she replied. Her words were a bit muffled with her head pressed against his chest.

"Did you miss the part where I said I loved you?"

"No." She leaned back and looked up at him. Her eyes were their bright blue, even with the rims red from all the smoke in the air. "I need you to tell me again."

"I love you."

She pressed a kiss to his lips. "And again. You can never tell me enough."

"I love you, now and forever."

Chapter Twenty-Five

A bird chirped a little melody somewhere in the distance. Warmth spread across her skin. The scent of blooms was in the air. Not incense — fresh flowers were in the room with her. Sophia reached out, spreading her arm across the bed and smiling as her hand came in contact with the muscular arm and torso of her husband.

"Hemi," she murmured.

"Yes, princess."

She still hated that damn nickname, but knew he called her that because he loved her. She was so certain in his adoration, because every day since he'd ended that sludge-sack's life and saved her, he'd done his best to prove it.

"Do we have to go to the race today?"

They'd been working so hard over the last two months to clean up Aurestral. The slave trade was officially stopped. The clubs were being revamped with none other than Artie in charge. She'd given up her position in Frog Lick for a chance at her own adventure. Though Sophia guessed Yuma had encouraged her, what with all the single, well-endowed men working them. But no more servitude for drugs, food and beds. No, Artie had plans to turn those clubs into a major flash asset for Aurestral — the first tourist spot on Mars.

Then the rooftop airponics gardens had launched with the hydroponics rehaul. Everywhere she looked there was another thing to improve. Schools for the children, investment in animals with fur that could be turned into clothing.

The days were long, and the nights… The nights were glorious. This was the first day in she couldn't remember how long that they didn't have a pressing issue or gang-related obligation to take care of. She wanted a chance to bask in lovemaking with her husband.

"We have to. I promised Drag. They have a shot with him behind the wheel."

Sophia sighed and rolled over, draping herself across Hemi's body. The sheet slid down and her nipples were already hard thanks to proximity.

"Then could we at least be late?"

Hemi lifted her up, dragging her until his lips could entangle with hers. She drank in those kisses and appreciated them like a glass of clean, fresh water. "That needy for me?"

"Do you blame me? We've been so busy, and I barely get any private time with you or I'm ready to pass out after one round on that fabulous cock of yours. I need more."

"Tell me what you want." Of course, he didn't stay still while waiting for her response. No, his hands started to wander, tweaking her nipples, his cybernetic fingers dipping between her thighs.

"I need you to finger-fuck me, then use your tongue, and after you're done, spear me with your fucking...oh," she moaned as he entered her. "That's good. Just like that."

He kissed her again, nice and slow as his cybernetic fingers moved at a faster pace. She'd never get enough of this, the way he worked her into a frenzy yet worshiped her mouth with reverence.

It wasn't long before she was panting and moaning. "I'm so close. Please, make me come."

"Your wish is my command."

Glossary

Airponics: Indoor greenhouse.

APU: Abbreviation for Allied Planetary Union. The governing body of all the planets in the Milky Way, except Earth, Earth's Moon, and Mars.

Aurestral: Affiliated Aurora territory gang-town.

Aurora: One of the three territories on Mars.

Auster: One of the three territories on Mars.

Barnabas: Affiliated Wespero territory gang-town.

BCS: Body Collection Service. An organization founded by the Allied Planetary Union that collects dead bodies for bone harvesting.

Bob-tailed scratcher: Possum-type animal with claws and bobbed tail.

Bone powder: Used to power the slip drive by mixing with water. Made from human bones. Most potent when mixed with urine as the acid mixes with the carbon molecules that light up more with electricity.

Bootleggers: Smugglers who run illegal booze from Earth to other planets.

Bumdum: Slang term for bummer.

Coon cat: A striped feral cat with a bushy tail.

Crinkle: Slang term for money.

Dust honey: Slang term for an attractive woman who lives on Mars and hangs around guys or gals in the hopes of gaining attention, money or notoriety.

Fatch: Alternative to the word fuck, in regional use by those from the Upper planets. Used alone or as a noun or verb in various phrases to express annoyance, contempt or impatience.

Flash: Slang term for money.

Fur-buns: Rabbit-type animal that lives in the wilds of Mars.

Gold leaves: Monetary currency, pressed gold in sheets as thin as leaves. Folks call it crinkle or flash depending on who they are and where they're from.

Goosemert: Mouse-like animal that burrows and lets out a honking wail.

Grav boots: Boots with a gravity lock built into the soles, designed for those who travel in space and may need to spacewalk.

Haulers: Four-seater coverless vehicles with a bed attached for hauling supplies or parts.

Holo-communicator: Handheld device used for talking to others, which can also project a 3D image of their face, if desired.

Holo-tablets: Handheld computers that can project images into the air in a 3D format.

Hover cycle: A motorcycle that hovers instead of having the wheels touching the ground.

Hydroponics: Water processing plant.

Inccukai: Elite assassins that were raised and trained to protect Allied Planetary Union Ambassadors. Some have left the order and taken jobs as freelance bodyguards and mercenaries. Often get their bodies enhanced with tech.

Joseph's balls: Curse slang term frequently used on the Lower Planets.

Klogs: People who lie about who they really are.

Kuargen: Affiliated Wespero territory gang-town.

Lower Planets: Earth and Mars.

Macintosh: Affiliated Wespero territory gang-town.

Marsanium: Iron-based ore mined on Mars and used to build ships.

Mars Racing Commission: Oversight committee that approves and monitors all racing activities on Mars.

Mars Shipping Commission: Oversight committee that approves and monitors all ship-building and mining activities on Mars.

Moonie: Slang term for those who live on Earth's moon.

MP: Mars Protectorate.

NiteOx: Deadly fuel-enhancing gas discovered in 2330.

Nkosi: Affiliated Wespero territory gang-town.

Osprerine: Affiliated Auster territory gang-town.

Recycle: Waste water processed and filtered for human consumption, but not as high quality as pure water.

Rising Sun: Affiliated Wespero territory gang-town.

Runners: Smugglers who run illegal drugs from Earth to other planets.

Scurdy: A scaredy-cat, someone who is afraid.

Skeiron: Affiliated Auster territory gang-town.

Silva-Chavez: Affiliated Wespero territory gang-town.

Singh: Affiliated Wespero territory gang-town.

Slip drives: Primary engines used by space-faring ships, which allow them to travel the currents in space.

Sludge: By-product of processed Marsanium that is used to fuel the racers on Mars.

Space fish: Slang term for someone who travels space, isn't familiar with planetary life or activities and tends to be impressed easily.

Space hole: A derogatory term, another way to say asshole.

Trolling engine: An engine powered by electricity that works in tandem with a ship's slip drive and can be used inside a planet's atmosphere and when moving short distances.

Uni-rider: A motorcycle-style bike that runs off Marsanium sludge.

Upper: A person who lives on an Upper planet.

Upper planets: Jupiter, Saturn and Neptune, including their moons.

Wespero: One of the three territories on Mars.

Zephyr: Affiliated Auster territory gang-town.

Want to see more from this author? Here's a taster for you to enjoy!

Full Throttle Cyborgs: Drag Me Down
Landra Graf

Coming December 2023

Excerpt

Dakota 'Drag' Michelson had always believed in two things. The first was that good always triumphed. Today was no exception.

"Full Throttle has cemented themselves in Wespero history by winning a regional trial race—not once, but twice!" Snapper roared over the crowd gathered in the Watering Hole, hoisting a large mug of house brew in the air in his cybernetic hand. The metal gleamed in the low light of the room. Drag's second-in-command stood on the small stage, a plywood platform that lifted folks about a half a foot off the ground and typically hosted music acts.

"They said we wouldn't do a repeat, but our fearless leader…Drag!"

Everyone looked at him. Over a hundred pairs of eyes were staring him down and he felt pinned in place. His feet were locked to the floor by a silent fear that made it impossible for him to move as he leaned against the bar. He'd never been big on attention, afraid they might find a flaw in his abilities. He managed to lift up his own mug in acknowledgment.

A deafening cheer erupted throughout the room, and Drag closed one eye as the noise hit his audio cortex just right to send a screech through his entire body. As if the sound had triggered the nanites in his system to have an adverse reaction and his nerves were momentarily revolting.

"Drag led us to victory," Snapper continued between drinks. "Just as he has since the moment we voted him leader of Frog Lick, leader of our gang. We celebrate tonight to remember how far we've come, because tomorrow, we start working towards the championship!"

Another roar rose through the room, paired with the clinking of glasses, the guzzling of brew and the jovial mood that no one could erase. This was the release of years of suffering. This gang had fought and clawed their way through poor engine designs, bad luck, explosions and losing their chance at an appeal with the Mars Shipping Commission.

No amount of presented evidence could convince that three-person board to commute or reduce the sentence they had handed down to Frog Lick three years prior. All courtesy of Bebe Smith, the previous gang-town leader, who'd been in a dirty deal with a terrorist cell from Earth's moon. They had almost launched an attack on the Uppers that would have made all of Mars suffer. The ruling groups of Mars had meted out the steepest punishment they could to show the Allied Planetary Union that they wouldn't let treason on such a scale happen again. But did Bebe suffer? No... She got locked away in a prison cell and fed. It was the people she left behind that ended up worse off.

Hard-working women, men and their children had suffered lack of food, support, and in some cases, much-needed medicine. They'd trusted in Drag and his close friends to help lead the way and direct their efforts.

Their labor, sleepless nights and even repeated loss had been worth it to inspire them to this moment. This town had even flourished, becoming the place of his childhood dreams. No one went hungry. Not a single person froze because they didn't have proper housing. Everyone who wanted to learn was allowed to. There were no longer gender lines for jobs.

Drag dared a glance at Gaia, their bartender and another close confidant. Her long pale blonde braids were wrapped up in twin buns at the back of her head. She wore a smile that didn't quite meet her pale gray eyes as she filled more mugs with brew and handed them off to one of the staff to distribute.

As if his stare had called to her, she sauntered in his direction. "You're awfully quiet for a man who should be on top of the world."

"We're not finished until we win the championship." They had put him in charge, expecting him to lead them to a future where their social standing or parental bloodline didn't matter. For that, they needed to assume the top reward gifted to gang-towns across Mars.

"Spoken like a man whose job is never finished. What then? When you win, how do you guarantee future success?"

He chuckled before swallowing a good amount of brew. "That's a problem for future me. Maybe you're right. I should be celebrating."

"Not a bad idea, considering we don't know what's on the horizon." Her words were soaked with the unspoken issues Full Throttle was dealing with outside of their win today. They were still without mining and ship building rights and on the brink of a turf war with a rival gang.

That woman will do anything to bury me.

The memory of bright red hair, sizzling green eyes filled with hatred and a physical touch that still seared his skin. He'd exorcised her plenty of times from his mind, sometimes with a body and other times with booze. Tonight he'd have to do more of the same.

"Care to help keep a man occupied?"

Gaia winked. "You know I don't mind a good spearing, but I've got other plans for tonight."

Drag didn't miss the bartender's gray gaze travel across the room to a black-haired woman with bright eyes and winsome smile. Also, a nice set of tits.

"Well, if you need a third—"

"I'll remember you, oh fearless leader. How about you interact with the people? I bet they'd love a rendition of the drive or any kind word about how you'll be leading us to victory." With that, Gaia left him alone and he was back to staring out among the crowd.

Snapper had come off the stage to be replaced by Privy, their local musician, who had already started to tune up his guitar and prepare to strum. Music would fill the room soon enough and give Drag a chance to slip away.

He turned around and leaned over the bar, rummaging with his human hand for a bottle of the good stuff he knew Gaia kept below. Emerging with amber-filled bottle, he let out a little grunt of appreciation for this, the finer things, and for this moment.

"Did you ever think we'd be here? Two years ago, stumbling across the shitty terrain, outlawed, outcast and both with absent right arms." Snapper's voice brought a grin to Drag's face.

The idiot was already three sheets to the breeze. He'd been celebrating the minute Drag crossed the finish line.

"Either your woman's going to have no use for you because you'll be too drunk to get it up or too annoying with all your reminiscing the good old days." Drag had already spent enough time in his head about the past today. He'd rather use the rest of celebration to forget.

"Don't talk about Gina like that. She can get me up any time, booze or not. My woman is the best."

"You're damn right."

Snapper pointed a cybernetic finger in his face. "Don't you forget it. Now I may have drunk too much, but damn it, I'm in a good mood. We deserve a win, right?"

They did. The music started, a bawdy jingle about racers and the dust honeys who loved them. The crowd cheered and some even started to join in. The lyrics were well-known and easily recited. This right here couldn't be found elsewhere, not with any other gang.

"Yes, but more than that, these people deserve the future we're trying to give him."

Snapper clapped a hand on his shoulder. "You're fucking right. I'm off to dance. Join us soon, don't wallow."

Drag tugged the stopper out of the bottle with his teeth, abandoning his now empty brew glass and opting to tag a swig straight from the bottle. Another swallow, another verse. The song and the booze were doing their job. Though he could vaguely recall another night this song had played, a time when he'd thought his path was headed in a completely different direction. One where he wouldn't be alone in his bed every night.

"Brother," said Rune's voice at his ear. Drag slapped the bar with his other hand in shock. He'd been so lost in his thoughts he hadn't seen Rune. His younger brother was a skinny, tanner and far nicer version of him. The kid had a wicked mind too, for agriculture and farming. He'd single-handedly helped Frog Lick survive after they had lost their primary source of income the last couple years.

"Come to give me a hard time about joining the celebration as well?" Drag could always count on Rune to hand things to him straight. His brother wasn't afraid to tell him when he might be pushing too hard or making a bad decision. Like Gaia and Snapper, Drag relied on Rune to be a voice of reason during his time as leader.

"I'm here because you have a visitor."

Drag smiled and downed another good gulp, letting the burn coat his throat. "Tell them to join the party."

"Afraid that might bring more attention to situation we don't want attention for. Might encourage you to stop downing that whiskey like recycle."

"Who the hell's out there? The Commission?" Hell, their racer had passed all the tests. Gina had triple checked everything, including their NiteOx conversion that made sure to follow all regulations. "If they're here to accuse us of cheating, tell them it's too late."

Rune leaned in and whispered in Drag's ear. "It's Bridget."

Drag immediately sobered and the glass of the bottle cracked in his hand, whiskey seeping out through the edges over his skin, cool and wet. "Where is she?"

"Outside. She wants to talk. To parlay, is what she said. Said you know what she meant, but I believe her. Only that Innkucai assassin is with her, no entourage."

Drag also believed no good deed went unpunished. So of course that bitch would show up now, in the middle of his moment of triumph. *She's a damn leech.*

"If I'm not back in one hour, get everyone outside and prepared for a fight."

"Are you sure that's a good idea?" Rune asked as he grabbed hold of the bottle in Drag's hand. "You can release the bottle."

"Good idea or not, if I'm not back, that means I'm dead or she is. Just be ready."

Because no interaction between them tended to end without someone hurt. The one conversation between them with Hemi present had been an exception. From the moment she'd betrayed him, this was the way things had gone. The only question was why the hell had she chosen to show up now?

About the Author

Landra Graf consumes at least one book a day, and has always been a sucker for stories where true love conquers all. She believes in the power of the written word, and the joy such words can bring. In between spending time with her family and having book adventures, she writes romance with the goal of giving everyone, fictional or not, their own happily ever after.

Landra loves to hear from readers. You can find her contact information, website details and author profile page at https://www.totallybound.com

Home of Erotic Romance

Sign up for our newsletter and find out about all our romance book releases, eBook sales and promotions, sneak peeks and FREE romance books!